"I've never found it easy to believe in the Maiden of Eagle Rock," she said, "not even after *being* the Maiden of Eagle Rock. I've always thought there was something a little sappy about her."

"Sappy!" Otis was puzzled. "What do you mean, sappy?"

"I mean her suicide. People have to be crazy to commit suicide. What's so great about a girl killing herself? Are we supposed to respect her for that?"

"It's a romance, Jemmy. It's a pretty story."

"I just wish that as long as I'm speaking to all of Minneapolis I was saying something besides 'Give up.'"

"What would you rather be saying?"

She thought for a moment. "I'd rather be saying '*Don't* give up.'"

Also by Jon Hassler

Adult Novels

STAGGERFORD

SIMON'S NIGHT

THE LOVE HUNTER

A GREEN JOURNEY

GRAND OPENING

Young Adult Novels

FOUR MILES TO PINECONE*

Published by Fawcett Books:

JEMMY

Jon Hassler

A Margaret K. McElderry Book

FAWCETT JUNIPER • NEW YORK

RLI: $\dfrac{\text{VL 6 \& up}}{\text{IL 7 \& up}}$

A Fawcett Juniper Book
Published by Ballantine Books
Copyright © 1980 by Jon Hassler

Library of Congress Catalog Card Number: 79-23091

ISBN 0-449-70302-9

This edition published by arrangement with Atheneum Publishers, A Division of Macmillan, Inc.

Chapters 1 and 2 of this novel appeared originally in Four Quarters, *a publication of La Salle College, Philadelphia.*

Manufactured in the United States of America

First Ballantine Books Edition: January 1989
Third Printing: June 1989

for M.

Chapter 1

O ut of the orange October sun rising over the reservation came an orange school bus heading for Eagleton. It swayed in the ruts of the gravel road and slowed to a stop where a short driveway led to the Stott place—a four-room house and a small shed huddled at the edge of the pine forest. The house and shed, bleached a pale blue by years of harsh weather, were tipped slightly toward each other; drawn together, it seemed, by the tight clothesline stretched between them. Parked in the weedy yard was an old Dodge the color of earth.

The bus driver honked. Jemmy Stott opened the kitchen door and hung a dishtowel on the clothesline, then, shivering, she went back inside for the denim jacket that hung on a nail by the door. As she walked slowly along the driveway the bus driver honked again, for he had ten miles and seventeen stops to go, but Jemmy did not hurry. Jemmy was always deliberate like this—not stubborn, merely deliberate—as though she had found, at seventeen, the pace designed for carrying a half-breed girl through a long, unpromising life. It was an all-purpose pace. When she swept the kitchen floor or smoked a cigarette or took a history test, she looked as though she were daydreaming; but despite her languid manner she always did a thorough

1

job of things: she swept in the corners, she smoked down to the filter, and she never flunked a test.

Jemmy's was a family of four. Her father was hooked on orange-flavored vodka and out of work. Her brother Marty was eleven years old, and her sister Candy was six. Her mother, a Chippewa, was dead.

Boarding the bus, Jemmy threw her long hair back over her shoulders and turned up the sleeves of her denim jacket to hide the tattered cuffs. She went to the back of the bus and sat, as usual, with Roxanne Rooster. Jemmy and Roxanne were thought of as friends, but the truth was that they didn't care much for one another. They had attended Reservation School together through the first eight grades and now they rode the bus together to Eagleton High School, but Roxanne (in Jemmy's opinion) was too loud and grabby. If Jemmy had two cigarettes, Roxanne wanted one. If Jemmy had one cigarette, Roxanne wanted half of it. If Jemmy had a new issue of *Bold Confessions*, Roxanne wanted to read it before Jemmy was done.

"Hi," said Jemmy as she sat down.

"Have you got any gum?" said Roxanne.

The honking of the school bus had awakened Jemmy's father. He sat up in bed and before he opened his eyes he put on a pair of glasses. His bed was in a windowless room not much bigger than a closet. He stood up and put on his pants and a flannel shirt, old and spotted with paint. All his clothes were spotted with paint because at one time he had been a house painter. Combing his faded red hair with the palms of his hands, he went barefoot into the living room, where Marty and Candy sat watching a fuzzy picture on TV. A cartoon man was chasing a cartoon cat. Or was it a dog? This far from the transmitter it was hard to tell. Marty and Candy sat on the bare floor with their jackets on.

"Come on," said Stott.

Marty and Candy pulled themselves away from TV,

2

looking back at it as they followed him into the kitchen. He found his shoes under the kitchen table and sat down to put them on.

The frayed denim jacket he shared with Jemmy wasn't hanging on the nail by the door. "Go out and get in the car," he said, and he went back to his bedroom for a paint-spotted sweater.

Marty ran out to the old Dodge and jumped into the back seat and locked all the doors. Candy ran after him, but she wasn't fast enough, and when she reached the car she couldn't get in. She hit the frosty window with her fist and shouted, "Damn you," and Marty laughed to hear her say it. He couldn't see out through the frost, but he knew by the slamming of the kitchen door that his father was coming, so he unlocked the doors and let Candy in.

Stott pressed the palms of both his hands on the outside of the windshield and melted away two patches of frost big enough to see through. Then he got into the car and started the engine and listened to it clatter for a minute before he shifted gears. He wrenched the steering wheel as far as it would go and turned in a tight circle between the shed and kitchen door. He drove out from the shadow of the house and turned east on the gravel road. The two clear patches on the windshield widened as he headed into the low sun, and by the time he had driven the two miles to Reservation School, the frost was sliding and dripping away from all the windows.

This was the first year that Stott had delivered his children to school. During the eight years that Jemmy had gone to Reservation School, she had walked the two miles every day. And Marty, too, had been accustomed to walking during his first four grades; but now Marty and Candy rode because this year Candy was old enough for school and she was Stott's favorite. Unlike Jemmy and Marty, Candy's hair was red, like her father's.

Reservation School had two outhouses and one teacher.

3

On the roof stood a belfry without a bell, and in the yard were two swings and a teeter-totter. As the engine of the Dodge idled and clattered, Stott watched Candy join a group of friends by the swings. The sight of her with other girls made him uncomfortable. She wore dresses of Jemmy's—third- and fourth-grade dresses from the days before girls wore jeans to school. They were too big for Candy and they reached nearly to her ankles. Stott saw that nobody else in the schoolyard looked so frumpy as Candy.

He made a U-turn and parked in front of Rooster's Store, which stood across the road from the school. In Rooster's Store you could buy groceries or hardware or chicken feed or get your shoes fixed or have a drink. The proprietor was a scar-faced Indian named Stan Rooster, who lived with his wife and two children (one of whom was Roxanne) in rooms behind and above the store.

"You're up early, considering last night," said Rooster. He smiled easily. His teeth were very large.

"So are you," said Stott, who seldom smiled.

Rooster chuckled, thinking how tipsy they had both been at two o'clock this morning when they had parted company.

Stott bought a pack of cigarettes.

"Coming back tonight?" asked Rooster.

"Not the way I feel right now."

"You'll be back." Rooster chuckled.

Stott returned home, and as he entered the kitchen he heard a TV voice speaking to the empty front room. He dropped his pack of cigarettes on the kitchen table and his sweater on the floor and he went to his bedroom for the bottle of orange-flavored vodka he kept under his bed. He had a breakfast of vodka and smoke, then he cleared a tangle of bedclothes off the couch in the front room (Marty's bedclothes, for the couch was Marty's bed) and he lay down to watch the fuzzy picture on TV. Before long he was asleep, and because he slept until late afternoon, Marty and

4

Candy (she for the first time in her six weeks as a first grader) walked home from Reservation School.

The orange bus brought Jemmy home from Eagleton at suppertime. The sun was low, and as she walked to the house a cold wind clutched at her open jacket and her long black hair. She shivered, but she did not hurry. From the woodpile behind the house, she carried into the kitchen a few sticks of dry pine and started a fire in the range. Her father was still asleep; Marty and Candy were watching TV. She picked her father's sweater off the floor and hung it, with her jacket, on the nail by the door.

Later, when she served up four plates of macaroni and called her family to the table, her father came into the kitchen with a headache. At the table, Marty was whistling loudly and Stott rapped him on the head with a spoon.

Halfway through the meal, Stott cleared his throat and fastened his eyes on the light bulb that hung on a cord over the table and said, "Jemmy, I want you to quit school."

Jemmy was pouring milk when he said it, and her hand did not falter.

"This is your twelfth year of school," he said, "and I don't see where it's getting us. I don't see the point in it. It's time you stayed home and took care of things full time. Candy needs somebody to get her ready in the morning. Get her fixed up decent. Drive her to school in the Dodge. I can't always be getting up at dawn, looking after the whole pack of you. It isn't good for my breathing, getting out in the cold air early in the morning. If the truth was known, I might be suffering from the same ailment your mother had, and she died of it."

Stott rarely said this much at one time, and Marty and Candy, wearing their jackets at the table, stopped eating and looked at him. He was speaking to the light bulb.

"So it's settled then. You've got the responsibility around here now. Take the car in the morning. Drop Candy and

5

Marty off at Reservation School, then go to town and quit. Half the kids your age around here quit a long time ago. I don't see the point in going to school all your life. Be sure you get a refund on your lunch ticket. And have four dollars' worth of gas put in the Dodge. They'll charge it at Texaco."

Stott brought his gaze down from the light bulb and glanced at Jemmy. Her eyes were on Marty and Candy, studying them, looking from one to the other as though she had never seen them before. And she hadn't—not in this light. If she understood her father correctly, Marty and Candy were now her responsibility. He was backing out. He was quitting his job as father just as he had quit painting houses. From now on, it was up to Jemmy.

"Well?" said Stott. He wanted her to reply. She would obey him, he knew, because that was her nature—slow, steady obedience. But he also knew that she was capable, on rare occasions, of anger. If she was going to lash out at him about this, he wanted her to do it now and get it over with.

"Well?" he said again.

"Well, what?" said Jemmy, and their eyes met for a moment. Then she stood and took her plate of macaroni to the garbage sack under the sink. She had lost her appetite. She filled the sink with hot water from the kettle on the range, and as she waited for the three of them to finish eating she gazed out the window, where dusk was creeping out of the dark forest.

"There's things to be done here," Stott said to the long black hair lying over her shoulders and down her back. "As soon as you quit tomorrow, get home and start shortening Candy's dresses. Nobody in first grade wears dresses as long as hers."

Jemmy did not turn away from the window.

"Nobody wears dresses to school but the teacher," said Marty, grinning.

"None of your lip," said Stott.

6

After supper Stott settled down on the couch in the front room to watch TV, but he couldn't rest easy. He wondered what Jemmy's silence meant. Was she building up steam until she exploded, like the time she caught him stealing cigarettes from the bedroom she and Candy slept in? Or was she simply taking it in stride, the way she had taken her mother's death? He remembered standing in the cemetery two days after Candy was born. As the preacher blessed the open grave and the men let down the coffin, Stott looked at the faces of Jemmy, eleven at the time, and Marty, five. Neither of them shed a tear. Nor did anyone else, for that matter. The faces of his wife's relatives—Chippewas all—were expressionless. Stott himself had no relatives that he knew of. As for his own sorrow, he did not reveal it in the cemetery, but saved it for later that evening when he could do it justice in Rooster's Store with his bottle of orange-flavored vodka.

From the couch Stott heard the rattle of dishes in the kitchen and he concluded that Jemmy was taking it in stride. Still, he couldn't relax. If only she would say something. He rose from the couch and hurried through the kitchen, where Jemmy was slouched over the dishwater, absently washing a plate, and Mary and Candy were kicking each other under the table. He took the denim jacket off the nail by the door and drove down the road to Rooster's Store.

Chapter 2

The next morning the ground was white with an inch of snow. Although it had stopped falling by the time Jemmy got up and dressed and cooked oatmeal, she could tell by the low sky over the forest that there was more snow to come.

When the school bus arrived, she waited in the kitchen while the driver honked four times and drove away. Then she called Marty and Candy away from TV. She put on the denim jacket and followed them outside. Marty ran to the car and locked the doors. Candy pounded on the window and said, "Damn you!" Jemmy brushed snow from the windshield and peered in at Marty. She said, "Unlock the doors this minute."

From the back seat Marty crossed his eyes and stuck out his tongue.

Jemmy unlocked the car with her key, then reached into the back seat and slapped Marty's cheek.

"Half-breed!" he screeched, his cheek stinging. He bounced on the seat, grinning, too proud to rub his cheek, and he ducked when Jemmy swung at him again.

"Half-breed!" he shouted once more, knowing that "half-breed" must be an insult because he felt hurt whenever he himself was called "half-breed" by the Indian kids in Reservation School and by the white kids who sometimes came partridge hunting in the forest behind the house. Again he ducked as Jemmy took another swing at him.

When Jemmy started the car, Marty relaxed. Then, with the engine idling, she shot her hand over the seat and grabbed him by the shirt. He struggled and shouted as she dragged him into the front seat and out the door and dropped him in the snow. She got back into the car and drove away, Marty running to catch up and cursing as he lost ground.

At Reservation School Jemmy let Candy out and said, "No reason you can't walk home this afternoon. The walk never hurt me, not even in first grade."

Candy stood beside the car, looking back down the road at Marty, a dark speck in the snowy landscape.

"Get going now," said Jemmy. She watched Candy, in a long dress, and Candy's girl friends, all in jeans, file into the schoolhouse.

She turned the car around and drove back the way she had come, toward Eagleton. Marty, scuffing along in the snow, saw her coming and stuck out his tongue and crossed his eyes. Jemmy stepped on the brake and gave him a threatening look and he scampered off toward school.

She did not park near the high school. She had never driven to school before and she was afraid that Morrie Benjamin and his gang, watching her arrive in the old Dodge, would make fun of her. Exactly what they would have found to ridicule, she wasn't sure, but they would have found something. Anything out of the ordinary was cause for Morrie Benjamin's mocking laughter. He was continually on the lookout for the unexpected—a girl's new hair style, an athlete on crutches—and when he found it he made it the object of his derision. Jemmy left the car on Main Street and walked to school.

The halls of Eagleton High were crowded and she had to force her way through the loud tangle of students to her locker. She opened the padlock and drew out her purse. It was a large leather purse with long fringes and a shoulder strap. She had bought it the previous year with her lunch money (she had skipped lunch for twenty-eight days), but she never took it home for fear of what her father might say. He never wanted her to have anything new. "A welfare check doesn't allow for foolishness," he always said. So during the past summer, rather than keep the purse at home, she had lent it to Roxanne Rooster. This fall when Roxanne reluctantly gave it back, the fragrance of leather had been replaced by the smell of cosmetics.

She hung the denim jacket in the locker, hung her purse over her shoulder, and went to the principal's office.

"I have to quit school," she said to the secretary, who was examining a dozen pencils in a neat row on her desk.

"Have you seen the nurse?"

"No," said Jemmy.

The secretary carefully selected the sharpest pencil and scratched her scalp with it. "See the nurse first," she said. "Then come back. The nurse has to clear you."

Through the open door behind the secretary Jemmy could see the principal sitting at a littered desk, a phone to his ear. This was the man who spoke each year to the Indian assembly and to the white assembly. He was a worried-looking man with gray hair and a gray face and a lot of loose flesh under his chin. "Please come to school every day," he begged every September at the Indian assembly. "Skipping school reduces our share of federal and state money. Skipping school causes great harm to your education." There was such anguish in his voice when he spoke of hit-and-miss attendance that the Indians were embarrassed. They didn't want to be the cause of anguish in a grown man. Steady attendance was out of the question for most of them. School wasn't all that compelling when there was wild rice to harvest or muskrats to trap or fish to net. So as soon as they were old enough (sixteen) they quit school altogether,

10

putting an end to their hit-and-miss attendance and (they hoped) to the principal's anguish.

Because Jemmy was a half-breed and because she lived near, but not on, the reservation, she was required each year to attend the white assembly as well as the Indian assembly. At the white assembly the principal pleaded not for good attendance (the whites hardly ever skipped) but for what he called "Indian empathy." "They come from a different culture and they haven't had your advantages," he told the whites, and Jemmy. "They come from a different background altogether, and we must try to empathize with them so that they will empathize with us. And when they empathize with us they will begin to adopt our values and they won't skip school, and when they quit skipping school our state and federal income will increase." Each white was asked to single out a particular Indian to empathize with. This was not something you had to declare out loud, but in your heart. Secretly you should decide which Indian you were going to get to know better, then pledge yourself to that Indian.

Jemmy had been tempted to pledge herself to herself. If she was expected to be two people at these assemblies, an Indian in the morning and a white in the afternoon, wouldn't it make sense for the Indian half of her to come to a better understanding of the white half? And vice versa? The idea amused her. And it confused her. If you were a member of two races, you didn't seem to have full membership in either. Being half Indian and half white didn't seem to add up to one total person; you remained two half persons. On the bus, Jemmy had tried to explain this to Roxanne Rooster, stressing the amusing part of it because whenever a discussion got serious Roxanne lost interest. She told Roxanne that when the principal asked each student to pledge herself to an Indian, she decided to pledge herself to herself. But Roxanne didn't think this was funny. She said, "Are you nuts?"

In his office the principal put down the phone and looked up at Jemmy as she stood at the secretary's desk. The sight of Jemmy disturbed him. Her clothes didn't fit. Her blouse was a size too small and her jeans were unfashionably short, and what were those things on her feet? Moccasins or slippers? They were so scuffed and dirty it was hard to tell. She had a pretty face, he thought, but her hair was stringy. A girl like that was a disgrace to Eagleton High School. What were the home-ec teachers doing with their time anyhow, that a girl her age should come to school that sloppy? And the health teachers. Wasn't a girl's health teacher supposed to keep her presentable?

The secretary handed Jemmy a hall pass. She left the office and the principal shook his head like a man in pain.

In the nurse's office a girl younger than Jemmy sat at a desk snapping her bubble gum. She looked Jemmy over.

"I'm supposed to see the nurse," Jemmy said. "I have to quit school."

"You seen a doctor?" the girl asked, her eyes on Jemmy's stomach.

"No."

"Nurse ain't in. Be in at nine thirty." The clock behind the desk said eight thirty.

"Either sit down and wait or get to your first-hour class," the girl said around her gum. "You got those two choices. I report misconduct. I belong to Future Teachers of America."

Jemmy left the office. The halls were empty now, the lights reflecting off the floor of polished tile.

In the rest room Roxanne Rooster was looking at her pimples in a mirror. Jemmy came in and they glanced at each other in the mirror but said nothing. If Jemmy's eyes weren't so pretty—naturally pretty—Roxanne would have liked her better. Jemmy stepped into a compartment and latched the door. She dug a cigarette out of her purse and waited to hear Roxanne leave before she lit up. Roxanne went to the door and pretended to leave, then when she heard the striking of the match she went into the compartment next to Jemmy's and said, "Give me one and I won't tell."

Jemmy had no choice. She handed a cigarette under the partition. She didn't mind giving away a cigarette, that was no great loss, but she hated being outwitted by Roxanne.

"Give me two and I won't tell," said Roxanne.

"I've only got one more besides the one I'm smoking. Go beg from somebody else."

"Give me half of it then."

Jemmy reached into her purse for her last cigarette. She tore it in two, and handed half under the partition. She put the other half back in her purse. Actually a cigarette and a half wasn't bad for a full hour of peace and quiet. She was supposed to be in history this hour. It wasn't a bad class—it was taught by the only teacher she liked—but Morrie Benjamin was in that class and he always said embarrassing things to Jemmy and he said them loud enough for the whole class to hear. In the rest room she could rest.

She said, "What class are you supposed to be in?"

"No class," said Roxanne. "I'm working in the lunch room this hour. I get free lunch for working."

They puffed in silence, smoke rising from the two compartments.

Jemmy said, "I'm quitting school today."

"I know it. I knew it first thing this morning. I told the bus driver, but he didn't believe me till he honked four times and you never came out."

"How did you know?"

"Because your dad told my dad last night in the store."

Another long silence. Then, hearing Roxanne leave her compartment, Jemmy said, "I don't mind quitting. It's all right with me."

Ready to leave the rest room, poised for a quick getaway, Roxanne said, "My dad says your dad needs you at home because he's drunk all the time and he can't even feed himself. Half-breed!" She hurried out the door.

Jemmy leaped from her compartment and ran to the door as it was closing and shouted, "Squaw!" into the hallway. She saw the principal standing out there. She pushed the door shut.

Roxanne reappeared at the door and called to Jemmy. "The principal wants to see you. He says come out."

Jemmy ran water over her cigarette, dropped it into the towel basket, and stepped out into the hall.

"Were you smoking in there?" The principal's gray jowls quivered.

Jemmy gave him a guilty smile.

"Yes or no?"

Jemmy nodded, smiling. Roxanne slipped around a corner and ran to the lunch room.

The principal's expression was closer to agony than to anger. "Have you ever taken home ec?"

Jemmy nodded.

"Well, what about health?"

Jemmy nodded.

"This year?"

"I had health every year."

He couldn't very well ask why if she had had these courses she looked such a mess, but that's what he wanted to know. Instead he asked, "Where do you belong this hour?"

"History."

"Whose history?"

"Olson's."

"*Mister* Olson's."

She nodded.

"Get to class then. You're late."

As she hitched up her purse strap and turned to leave, he said, "Why do you Indians cause me so many problems?"

"I'm half Irish," said Jemmy.

14

Mr. Olson was writing on the blackboard as Jemmy opened the door and crossed the front of the room to her desk. Morrie Benjamin, whose desk was across the aisle from hers, said, "Look at that wiggle." The class laughed. Morrie had a well-kept mustache and a cool lift of his brow, which gave him, at seventeen, an undeserved reputation for wisdom. He was the wit of first-hour history.

Mr. Olson turned from the board and told Morrie to be quiet.

"But Mr. Olson," said Morrie, wearing the expression of mock-seriousness he was so good at, "Jemmy's wiggle is going down in history. It's known as the American Indian Movement." The class laughed for nearly a minute.

Rather than try to raise his voice above the noise, Mr. Olson waited it out. He was a small man, always perfectly dressed. He habitually clutched the lapels of his suit coat as though trying to draw himself to a height greater than his five and a half feet. Though this class gave him little to smile about, Jemmy had been in other classes of his and liked his gentle nature—a kindly man so unlike her father that he was often on her mind, like a friend.

"All right, settle down," he said when he judged that he could be heard. But he couldn't. As he waited for the noise to subside, he looked at Jemmy. She smiled at him. She never looked at him without smiling.

Finally when the laughter wore out, he pointed to the board and said, "Copy this name in your notebooks. Otis Chapman is one of our leading American painters, and he has been commissioned to paint a huge mural in downtown Minneapolis commemorating our Indian heritage. He is currently in our area doing studies for this mural."

As he turned to write more on the board, Morrie leaned across the aisle and snatched Jemmy's purse from under her desk. Tormenting Jemmy was one of his hobbies. Since he had begun dating Roxanne Rooster, certain people had been calling him an Indian lover, and abusing Jemmy was his way of demonstrating that his love for Roxanne did not extend to the entire Chippewa nation. He handed the purse to Sam Forster, who sat behind him. Sam, instead of passing it down the aisle as Morrie expected, turned it upside down and emptied it over Morrie's head. Morrie was humiliated. He swung around and punched Sam in the nose. Mr. Olson turned from the board in time to see Sam tumble out of his desk and to see Jemmy claw at Morrie's face. She stung Morrie's cheek, but her fingernails were chewed too short to draw blood. The class laughed like hyenas. In an attempt to regain the limelight from Sam and Jemmy, Morrie turned to face the class and crossed his eyes. The class howled, but Jemmy didn't think this was funny. It was the same cross-eyed expression that Marty was so fond of, and Marty was only eleven.

Sam Forster rose from the floor and hurried out of the room, trying to hold the blood in his nose. At the sight of blood, the class was suddenly quiet, giving Mr. Olson the opening he needed for his lecture on behavior, which they had all heard before.

As he spoke, Jemmy knelt on the floor putting things back in her purse—a tube of lipstick, a comb, car keys, half a cigarette. She couldn't find her coin purse, which contained the grocery money her father had given her from his welfare check. It had fallen from the purse into Morrie's lap. She had not seen Morrie put it in his pocket.

After history class, Jemmy pressed herself through the crush of students to the nurse's office. The Future Teacher, blowing a bubble, pointed to an inner room, where Jemmy found the nurse sitting at her desk. She was a woman of fifty with a carefully made-up face and a high pile of blue hair, to which was pinned a tiny white cap like a toy sailboat.

"Yes?"

"I'm supposed to see you. I have to quit school."

16

The nurse stood up and came around her desk with her arms outstretched. "My poor girl. Come and sit down. Have you seen a doctor?"

"No."

The nurse drew Jemmy to a bench and sat down with her arm around her shoulder. "We'll make an appointment. I know how troubled you are. I see it in your face."

This surprised Jemmy. She didn't feel particularly troubled. So far, this school day was no more troublesome than a lot of others.

"Talking about it openly is the best way." The nurse gave Jemmy a benevolent smile. "Any number of girls will tell you it's best to talk about it. Keeping it a secret is not the solution. Now let's take it one step at a time. Will the boy marry you?"

"What boy?"

The nurse's smile faded and her eyes narrowed.

"Aren't you pregnant?"

Jemmy said she wasn't.

The nurse looked as if she had been deceived. "Why must you quit school?"

"I have to take care of the house and my brother and sister. My dad says."

The nurse sighed. "You have no mother to keep house?"

"No."

"Died? Or ran away."

"Died."

A pause.

"Do you want to quit school?"

Jemmy shrugged. Like her father, she too had wondered what she was doing in school beyond her sixteenth birthday. The routine of the school day seemed so childish. So meaningless.

"Do you want to keep house?"

"I don't care. Dad says."

"Don't be so pliable, girl. Don't go through life doing

17

what others tell you to do. This is the age of self-determination, particularly for women. And that goes for Indians as well as the rest of us."

Jemmy nodded. She assured the nurse that she would stand up for her rights. She didn't want to be the cause of unhappiness in the nurse as well as the principal.

The nurse returned to her desk and picked up a pen.

"What year are you?"

"Senior."

"How old?"

"Seventeen."

"Will you come back sometime and finish school?" She had to know in order to use an inter-office memo of the proper color—pink for temporary withdrawal, yellow for permanent.

Jemmy shrugged.

The nurse initialed a yellow slip. Indians seldom came back. She handed Jemmy the slip and said, "Why don't you Indians ever finish school?"

"Roxanne Rooster will finish," said Jemmy, hoping the nurse would be pleased.

The halls were empty and quiet again. Jemmy went to the principal's office with the yellow slip, and while the secretary searched the files for her school records, Jemmy again looked through the open door to the inner office. The principal was seated there at his desk and talking to someone Jemmy couldn't see. But she could hear what both men were saying, and she recognized the voice of Mr. Olson.

"I'm afraid my eight-thirty class is going down the drain."

"It's too early in the year to say that," said the principal. "Drains aren't open this early in the year." He laughed. Jemmy didn't hear Mr. Olson laugh.

"I've been with this class for six weeks and it never gets any better. It's my worst ever."

"Who's in it?"

"Morrie Benjamin. Sam Forster. That whole crowd."

"Familiar names. They have come to my attention. They're all capable of a little hell-raising now and then, but they're not all ringleaders. Find the ringleader and subdue him and your problem is solved."

"I know the ringleader. It's Morrie Benjamin."

"Then half your problem is solved. Now subdue him."

"How?"

"You're the teacher, you know your students better than I do. You know what there is about Benjamin that irritates you. Figure out an agreement you can both live with. Take the boy aside and strike a bargain."

Finding Jemmy's records, the secretary returned to her desk and typed the date on a card. "Gemstone Opal Stott?" she asked without looking up.

Jemmy said that was right, that was her name.

The secretary typed *Gemstone Opal Stott* next to the date, then typed *Withdrawal*. She handed the card to Jemmy. "Show this card to each of your teachers except study hall teachers and bring it back signed by all of them. Turn in your books to each teacher and clean out your locker. You will make restitution for books torn, written in, or otherwise damaged. You must get the signature of the librarian. If you ever return to school, you must enter under your present name. No name changes until after you re-enroll. Speak well of Eagleton High School and be grateful for what it has done for you."

"I've got half the punches left on my lunch ticket." Jemmy handed her lunch ticket to the secretary, who unlocked a cash drawer.

The principal was saying, "I haven't met a student yet who wouldn't negotiate. Except Indians. You can't negotiate with Indians because they never say anything."

"Negotiate! The agreement is that I am to teach

American history and the student is to learn American history. What is there to negotiate?"

"There's always a bargain to be struck, Olson. Last year we had Lloyd Harrison teaching here, you remember. Well, he had a kid in his class who kept him off-balance all the time. You know the kind of kid I mean—forever talking under his breath to no one in particular. But you've got to hand it to Harrison. He worked out what I call a reasonable compromise. He allowed the kid to sleep in class every day and the kid, in turn, agreed to be quiet every day, even when he wasn't sleepy. You see, the kid was bored with the class and he sought diversion by talking under his breath. But once he had permission to sleep, his boredom was no longer a problem. A bargain was struck."

Mr. Olson left the principal and hurried through the outer office. "I'm late for second hour," he said over his shoulder. He didn't notice Jemmy standing at the secretary's desk.

The principal came and stood in his doorway and called after him, "I could tell you about a case in Prairie City. I had a teacher named Purvis in Prairie City who could work out bargains with ringleaders on the first day of school."

Mr. Olson was gone, and the principal told the rest to the secretary, who was only half listening. "Purvis took the ringleader aside and talked it over. It was from Purvis I learned about bargaining with students. You might think I got it from books, but no, I got it from Purvis in Prairie City."

The principal noticed Jemmy. His face fell. "Not you again. Get to your second-hour class." He returned to his desk.

"Two sixty," said the secretary, counting out Jemmy's refund. "You might have to return it, and more, if you've lost any books. We lose more books to Indians than to anybody else."

Jemmy went to her locker and paged through her books,

20

removing papers from between the pages. Some of the papers were old assignments and tests and these she threw away. The rest were pencil sketches of trees and barns and flowers that she had drawn during dull classes and study hall. She studied the sketches one by one. Most she tore up and threw away, but the better ones she folded and stuffed into her purse.

Then she made the rounds, interrupting classes. Her remedial math teacher said good luck, her health teacher said good luck, her bookkeeping teacher said good luck, the librarian said nothing because talking wasn't allowed in the library, and her English teacher said good luck. All her teachers wore the same grim expression, as though Jemmy were a worry they would be glad to forget.

She saved Mr. Olson till last. He answered her knock and looked at the withdrawal card.

"You're quitting, Jemmy? Because of what happened in class this morning?"

"No, Dad says." She smiled.

"But you're a senior."

She nodded.

"He needs you at home?"

She nodded again.

"I hope it's the right thing you're doing." He signed the card and gave her the smile she had hoped for.

"Good luck," he said.

She returned to her locker and put on her jacket. She took the withdrawal card into the office and when she came out classes were changing again. It was ten thirty. She pushed her way through the warmth and noise and smell and jostling of high school and stepped outside into thick, muffling curtains of falling snow—large wet flakes so dense that all the sights and sounds along the street were fuzzy at the edges, and she could scarcely see where she was going.

21

Chapter 3

By the time Jemmy reached Main Street, her hair and shoes were soaked by the wet snow. She went into the Heap Big Discount Store and searched through a pile of two-dollar jeans on a sale table. She found a pair that appeared to be Candy's size. She had planned to buy a more expensive, more durable pair, along with some bread and milk from the grocery store, but she had lost her coin purse. She paid for the jeans with her lunch-ticket refund and had enough money left for a pack of cigarettes.

She crossed the street to the Dodge and cleared the windshield of snow. She started the engine, lit a cigarette, then backed away from the curb. Driving along Main Street, she decided that she would not go home the usual way. She would mark this special day—the end of her education—by taking a different route home. Morning and night for over three years she had traveled the bus route, looking at the same monotonous barns and fields and hills. Today, with the car, she was free to choose. She would take a road she remembered from the days when she and her mother used to go blueberry picking. It was a longer way and the road was narrow, but it was more interesting, for it followed the north bank of the Turtle Egg River and climbed a bluff called Eagle Rock and wound through a forest of giant Norway pines. It was a fifteen-mile route instead of the usual ten, but Jemmy was sure that if she made the right turns she would come out on the other side of the forest not far from her house.

Out in the country the snowfall seemed thicker. As long as she kept moving, the snow blew off the windshield, but when she stopped at crossroads to get her bearings it quickly piled up on the glass and she had to get out and brush it away, for the wipers had quit working years ago. She drove uphill to Eagle Rock, the wheels spinning in the muddy snow, and when she reached the crest she came to a stop. The view of the river valley from Eagle Rock was said to be breathtaking. As a little girl she had been here with her mother, but she could not remember the view. The falling snow muffled all sound except the clatter of the idling engine. She switched off the ignition and got out of the car. Now all was perfect silence. And perfect whiteness. Large, light snowflakes clung to Jemmy's eyelashes and turned to water. She walked to the edge of the cliff for a look at the Turtle Egg River far beneath her, but veils of slanting snow concealed it. She felt as though she were suspended in the sky, beyond sight of earth. She felt giddy. She knew that from where she stood it was a long drop to the rocky shore of the river, yet it seemed that if she stepped off the edge today she would be enfolded in feathers.

Suddenly at her right side there was a rush of air and a swirling of snowflakes and she caught sight, for an instant, of an eagle. It was a huge golden eagle sailing past her right shoulder and out over the river and banking gracefully into oblivion. She had seen eagles before but never this close. This one she could have touched. Its dark brown wings were as long as her arms. Its head was gold and its hooked beak ivory. She had seen the black pupil of its eye. She stood there for a long time, enjoying a sensation of weightlessness, of remoteness from the world, of hovering where eagles flew.

Descending from Eagle Rock, she drove for some miles

23

looking for landmarks from years ago when she last went berry picking with her mother. She recognized no landmarks. Had the snow obliterated them, or had she made a wrong turn? She drove a long way in a direction she assumed was east, though without the sun she couldn't be sure.

Finally she admitted to herself that she was lost. But she wasn't frightened. Where was the danger in becoming lost between Eagleton and home? All roads led somewhere. All roads leading into forests led out again. She had only to follow this one and she was sure to come to a farmhouse where she could ask directions.

She drove another mile, then the car coughed and jerked and stopped.

"Damn!" said Jemmy under her breath. The gas needle pointed to empty. She had forgotten to stop at the Texaco station.

She lit a cigarette and listened to the whirring of the clock on the dashboard. At home when her father wanted to know what time it was he would send one of the kids out to the car, for this clock, like the car's engine, had been running noisily and dependably for as long as Jemmy could remember. Now it said noon. In the time it took the second hand to make a complete circle, thick snow covered the windshield.

She would wait for a car to come along heading for Eagleton. She would hitch a ride to the Texaco station, pick up a can of gas, then hitch a ride back here to the car. Then she'd return the can to the station and set out once more for home—this time on the road she knew. She would arrive at Reservation School by the time Marty and Candy were let out. They shouldn't be made to walk home in this heavy snow. Her father needn't know that she had run out of gas. He would wonder why she had taken so long, and she would say, "It's not easy quitting school."

It was nearly one o'clock before a car came along, and

24

she missed it. With the snow covering the windshield, she did not see it approach, and by the time she jumped out and waved her arms, it was already far down the road and hidden by the snow that swirled up behind it. One ten. One fifteen. It was cold in the car. Jemmy stuffed the sack containing Candy's jeans into her purse. She got out of the car and locked it. She buttoned her jacket up to her throat, hung the purse over her shoulder and began walking toward Eagleton in the tire tracks of the car that had passed. But after a few steps she changed her mind. She turned around and walked in the opposite direction. She knew that miles of wilderness lay between her and Eagleton; perhaps ahead, over the next hill, she would find help.

Over the hill were a small house and a large barn. On a post near the driveway a sign said *Mean Dog*. The tire tracks she had been walking in came out of this driveway. She followed them up to the door of the house and knocked. No answer. She pounded harder, and a black dog with snow on its back came around the corner of the barn and looked at her sadly.

"Here, boy," said Jemmy, and the dog retreated, sideways, keeping a drooping eye on her until he was out of sight behind the barn.

Jemmy tried the door. It was unlocked. She put her head in and called and got no response. She stepped inside and looked for a telephone, but there was none, so she left, pulling the door shut tight. She set off down the road. She would see what lay over the next hill.

Now, with no tire tracks, it was harder walking. Her feet were wet and cold. A half mile further on, the road narrowed and wound through a stand of lofty pines whose branches arched over Jemmy's head. Here less snow was filtering through to the ground, and walking was easier. Now and then, high up in a tree, a bough of pine needles dipped and released a cascade of powdery snow. Jemmy recalled picking blueberries under trees like this. Maybe she wasn't lost after all.

The temperature seemed to be dropping. Her feet grew numb. She walked faster. The road wound left and right through the forest. She startled a covey of partridges—a dozen or more—and they thundered up from a bush beside the road and flapped away through the trees in a frantic, zigzag flight. Further on, she saw an antlered deer crossing the road ahead of her—a large buck. She stood still and watched him pick his way slowly through a tangle of fallen logs and branches and turn toward a clearing in the distance. Another deer crossed the road and followed him, then a pair, then a group of three, including a fawn, each stepping, it seemed, in the leader's hoofprints. Jemmy marveled at the grace of their movements and watched until the last flick of the last white tail blended into the snowy haze under the trees.

She hurried on and after several minutes she came to a landmark she recognized. Beside the road and surrounded by a rectangle of fenceposts was the stone cellar of a house long ago destroyed by fire. This was where her mother had always parked the Dodge when they picked berries. Every July this open cellar was their landmark. They would pick in opposite directions from it, and about noon the first one back to the car would honk the horn in case the other was lost or had forgotten what time it was. They would eat their picnic lunch beside this stone foundation. The sandwiches and the green shade and the sound of the breeze high in the pines always made Jemmy sleepy, and after lunch she would nap on the ground before picking berries in the afternoon. Some years she and her mother came home with all the pans and pails they owned full of blueberries. Other years they filled only a couple of bowls. To this day there were purple stains on the threadbare upholstery of the Dodge.

The sound of wind rose suddenly in the treetops, and Jemmy felt frightened. Wind made blizzards out of heavy snow. Wind piled up drifts too high to walk through. She hurried on, running and walking, and covered what seemed miles before the road emerged from the forest and ran between open fields and low swampland. Here Jemmy felt the wild force of the wind. It picked snow off the ground and sent it swirling high overhead. Her mother had often said that nature was the best friend you could have. She used to tell Jemmy that there were lessons in nature—all of nature—and if you paid attention to the sky and the trees and the rivers and the animals you could learn a lot about how to live your life. Jemmy had always had a hard time believing this, and now—with a blizzard building—her mother's words seemed foolish. Surely the wind and snow were enemies, not friends. The wind seemed to come from all directions at once, blowing snow in her face no matter which way she turned her head. She trudged through snow up to her knees, using a line of fenceposts as her guide. The ground and sky—everything but the fence line—blended into a white oneness.

The fence made a right-angle turn and Jemmy, turning with it, climbed a slope and found herself under a large tree. Beyond the tree was a building. Two buildings. Three. She headed for the nearest one and came to a door with a rusty latch. She opened the door and stumbled inside, pushing the door shut behind her. She was standing on a concrete floor in a dim, low-ceilinged passageway. She inhaled the warm smell of hay and manure. She leaned for a moment against the door and became aware, in the relative warmth of the barn, of how cold she had been. Snow had blown down inside the collar of her jacket, and her long black hair was tipped with ice. Wet snow was freezing on her sleeves and jeans. Her face and hands were numb.

In the light from a row of small windows, she saw a horse hang its head over the gate of a box stall. The ice on her jeans rasped as she walked over to the stall and opened the gate. She stepped inside and pressed her cold face against the horse's warm neck. She held her fingers under his nostrils. The horse was not uneasy. He was too old to be skittish. He stood quietly, exhaling puffs of steam from his large flabby muzzle and brought feeling back into Jemmy's hands. Then out of curiosity he turned his head to look her in the eye.

Jemmy glanced about, expecting to see or hear other animals, but there were none. She saw a pen for pigs and stanchions for cows, but the barn's only occupant was this old horse. Whoever lived on this farm must have sold all the livestock and retired, thought Jemmy. She imagined an elderly couple sitting idly in the farmhouse. But *was* there a farmhouse? She hadn't noticed. Should she go back outside and look for a house, knock on the door, and ask for help? That would be risky. Living around here were many people who disliked Indians. Some of the least tolerant, in fact, were the elderly. The expressions of disdain and suspicion that Jemmy attracted on the streets of Eagleton were often on the faces of old people. Of course on a day like this who would be so cruel as to turn a lost traveler away? Probably no one, no matter what he thought of Indians. Still, Jemmy felt safer with the horse, whose body heat would keep her warm enough to survive until the wind went down. Better to feel welcome in a chilly barn than to be given the cold shoulder in a warm house.

Suddenly the barn door opened and closed. A light came on and, with it, a radio. Jemmy crouched behind the horse, out of sight. She feared being found in the barn, for she knew that white people were very strict about keeping strangers off their property. There were laws against trespassing. Jemmy watched someone in overalls walk past the stall and climb the ladder at the far end of the passageway.

The radio played music, and then a voice said that the weather report was next, sponsored by Gene's Food Market in Eagleton. Obviously this had once been a dairy barn, thought Jemmy. She had picked up a lot of farming lore during her three years on the school bus, and she knew that dairy farmers usually kept a radio on during milking time because the noise helped put the cows at their ease. And since there were seldom any wall plugs in old barns, the radio was wired into an overhead socket and came on with the lights.

"Heavy snow and wind continuing through the night," said the radio. "A traveler's warning has been issued for the entire state of Minnesota. Temperatures will drop to a low of zero Fahrenheit by morning. Schools in the Eagleton area have already closed so that rural students may reach home while the roads are still passable."

Jemmy heard footsteps above her in the hayloft. In the ceiling over the stall a trapdoor opened. A bundle of hay dropped down beside the horse, and a voice—a woman's voice—said, "There's your supper, old Socko." The trapdoor closed.

The woman in overalls descended the ladder and said as she passed the stall, "We'll have to bring you water from the house, Socko. The faucet out here is frozen shut." The light and radio went off. The door opened and closed.

Jemmy moved over and sat down in the hay. She covered her legs with it. Her feet stung as they warmed. So did her face. The stinging in her face was very painful, worse than in her feet. Her cheeks had been sensitive to the cold since the day in the third grade when she froze them walking home from Reservation School.

She rested her back against the wall and listened to the slow grinding of Socko eating supper. He ate most of his hay, but not the hay that covered Jemmy's legs. He seemed to understand that she needed it more than he did, and instead of uncovering her he went nosing about in the corners of the stall, looking for shreds of hay from his last meal.

The light and the radio came on again. This time a man

29

with a black beard approached the stall. He carried a heavy pail, which he set on the floor and pushed under the bottom bar of the gate.

"Here's your water, Socko. It's on the warmish side so it won't freeze so fast."

Jemmy peeked at the man from where she sat in the shadows behind the horse. She couldn't see his face clearly because the light was behind him, but he didn't appear old enough to be a retired farmer. His actions were vigorous and quick, like those of a younger man.

Socko put his head into the pail for a drink, and the man walked away. The radio announcer was still speaking of the weather: "Much colder tonight. Temperatures below zero Fahrenheit by morning." Jemmy moved to a more comfortable position, and then, looking up, she saw that the man was back, holding a basin over the top rail of the stall.

"Here's your oats, old boy," he said—then he caught sight of Jemmy. Startled, he dropped the basin and took a step backward. Jemmy jumped to her feet and said, keeping the horse between them, "I only came in to warm up. I was walking and got lost."

The man came forward to the gate, peering at her with a scowl. It was a frightening look, and Jemmy said, "I'll be going now, and I won't bother you again. I just came in to get warm."

"Nobody's going anywhere in weather like this," he said, opening the gate and reaching for her hand. "Come to the house, where it's warm." His voice was reassuring— deep and gentle. After a moment's hesitation Jemmy stepped around the horse.

The man looked her over. "Your clothes," he said. "They're all wet and icy." He took her hand and drew her quickly from the stall and shut the gate. "My wife will find you some dry clothes. Come on."

With her hand in his, Jemmy feld suddenly exhausted, as though she couldn't have taken another step without his help. He guided her from the barn and across the yard. She was surprised to see the afternoon already darkening to a dusky blue. Her mother used to say that it got dark early on days like this because the wind blew a hole in the sky and let the daylight drain away. As they approached the door of the house, the wind rose fiercely and lashed her face with her ice-tipped hair. The man opened the door and led her into a large kitchen. On one wall was a stone fireplace, where the woman in overalls was feeding wood to the flames.

The man said, "Ann, look what the blizzard brought us."

The woman turned. Her first reaction was to draw back slightly, as the man had done in the barn; then she hurried to Jemmy's side, saying, "Good lord, you're freezing," and she led Jemmy to a chair in front of the fire. She knelt at Jemmy's feet and removed her icy shoes. Then she brought a bundle of her own clothes, showed Jemmy to a bathroom, and told her to change.

Shyly, Jemmy returned to the kitchen, wearing the woman's slacks and sweater and slippers.

"You're shivering," said the woman. "Come to the fire." She led her again to the chair. She studied Jemmy's face and said, "Otis, look at her cheeks. They're so pale. There's something wrong with them."

"It's frostbite," said Jemmy. "It's nothing to worry about."

The man touched her cheeks gently with his fingertips. He said, "Maybe we should call a doctor."

"I've had frostbite before," said Jemmy. "It's nothing." She put her hands to her face and trembled with cold. And with self-consciousness. She wished they would quit staring at her.

"Look, there's a purple spot on her right cheekbone," said the woman. "Otis, we must call a doctor."

The man, Otis, went to a phone that hung on the wall near the kitchen table and called a doctor in Eagleton. Their conversation was brief. Otis thanked the doctor and hung up.

"He says if she has feeling in her face there's probably no danger." Otis peered, frowning, into her eyes. "Do you have feeling?" he asked.

Jemmy nodded. She had feeling all right. For the next half hour or so it was the worst pain she had ever endured. It kept her from making much sense when the man and woman asked her questions. They wanted to know who she was and where she lived and how she happened to be lost in the storm.

"I'm Jemmy Stott. I live on County Road Nine two miles this side of the reservation. I was driving home from Eagleton and ran out of gas." She stopped short of telling them she had quit school. They looked like the kind of people who wouldn't approve.

"I'll call your parents and tell them you're safe," said Otis. "What's your number?"

"We haven't got a phone," said Jemmy. "But I better call Rooster's Store and see if my little brother and sister got home all right. Can I use your phone?"

"Of course." They backed away to let her out of the chair. She looked up Rooster's number and dialed hesitantly. In her seventeen years she had made no more than half a dozen phone calls.

Roxanne answered. She said that Marty and Candy were staying with the Roosters overnight. Roxanne called to Marty and Candy and both of them shouted something unintelligible into the phone. Jemmy asked them to repeat it, but they were overcome with giggles and couldn't speak.

"It's me again," said Roxanne. "Did you know that since you quit school I'm the only Indian girl left in the senior class?" There was triumph in her voice, as though Jemmy's presence in classrooms all these years had delayed Roxanne from achieving her ambition in life. "And I'm full-blooded," she added.

"Good-bye," said Jemmy.

Now it was suppertime. The woman in overalls served bowls of stew and large rolls and tried to make conversation, but Jemmy—exhausted from her trek through the snow and dazed now by the warmth of the kitchen—grew weak and sleepy at the table and was only vaguely conscious of being helped upstairs to bed.

Chapter 4

In the kitchen behind Rooster's Store, Mrs. Rooster served pizza and root beer for supper. Stan Rooster, as usual, took his portion into the store and sat down in the easy chair that stood between the bread rack and the beer cooler. This was where Stan Rooster ate all his meals, for he kept the store open from early morning till late in the evening and he liked to be on hand if customers dropped in. Tonight, of course, there would be no customers because everyone was snowbound, but he ate here anyway, out of habit.

Rollie Rooster and Marty Stott took their plates into the living room. They sat on the linoleum in front of the TV and waited for the evening news to be replaced by something more interesting. This was color TV, and like most things in the Rooster household, it made a great impression on Marty. How wonderful, he thought, to have pizza for supper and to be able to eat it on the living room floor in front of a color TV. How lucky to have a store built right onto the front of your house, with all the free candy and pop. Marty turned to look through the doorway into the kitchen and saw his sister Candy sitting at the table with Mrs. Rooster and Roxanne. How lucky to have a sister like Roxanne, who never seemed to give orders the way Jemmy did. He studied Mrs. Rooster, who was laughing at something Roxanne was saying. What a curious thing was a mother.

Mrs. Rooster was fat and good-natured, and although it was obviously hard work to move her great bulk from one room to another, she kept the house and store clean and her family well fed. She was usually ignored by her husband and disobeyed by her children, yet she seemed constantly in a good humor. Now, still laughing, she was patting Candy on the head. Roxanne lit a cigarette.

Marty turned back to the TV. He liked having Rollie Rooster at his side. The very best thing about being snowbound with the Roosters—even better than the pizza and the mother and the color TV—was the chance to spend the night with Rollie. Rollie was a seventh grader, and the seventh grade represented, to Marty, a very high station in life. In school the seventh graders sat in the large desks at the back of the room and at recess they outran you and outclimbed you and taught you dirty words and then when things got dull they beat you up. To be a seventh grader's friend was a privilege.

Though Marty didn't know it, Rollie was pleased to have Marty as his guest. He liked the mischief he saw in Marty's eyes. Rollie had a reputation as a hell-raiser. He was, in the words of the teacher, Miss Frost, a behavioral challenge. Until now, Rollie had carried out his pranks alone, but he was considering going into partnership, and it struck him that perhaps Marty Stott, although younger and only a half-breed, was the accomplice he had been looking for.

Most of Rollie's pranks had been directed against the single greatest curse in the world—school. Because he lived across the road from Reservation School, he had been able to accomplish things quickly and secretly under the cover of darkness, and when Miss Frost and the school board put their heads together to investigate the vandalism, Rollie was never the prime suspect. The prime suspects were older boys from distant parts of the reservation, boys with cars and worse reputations than Rollie's. Since the opening of school this year, Rollie had painted seven forbidden words on the side of the schoolhouse facing the road, he had tipped over both outhouses, he had plugged the chimney and smoked out a meeting of parents, and he had run a pair of his sister's underpants up the flagpole.

Rollie had never spoken of these pranks to anyone, but tonight as they sat before the TV he spoke of them to Marty. He called them jobs. He asked if Marty was interested in doing jobs like that. And of course he was.

"Super," said Rollie. "We'll do our first job tomorrow morning."

"What will we do?" asked Marty.

"We'll break into the schoolhouse."

By morning the blizzard had passed. Marty and Rollie rose with the sun, scraped the ice off the bedroom window, and looked down at the bright stillness that follows a blizzard. The snow was almost too dazzling for the eyes. The road and the roadside fenceposts were buried in drifts. No school today, certainly, for it would be several hours before the snow plows from Eagleton worked their way out to the reservation. Across the road the snowdrifts were as high as the window sills of the school, but the roof of the school was bare of snow, having been swept clean by the wind. In the entire landscape, the only sign of life was a cluster of sparrows perched in the belfry.

The boys were the first ones downstairs. They went into the store.

"Do what I do," said Rollie, slipping a pack of cigarettes into his pocket.

Marty took two packs.

"Do what I do," said Rollie, stuffing several candy bars into another pocket.

Marty grabbed a handful of candy bars, then went back for a third pack of cigarettes.

"Follow me," said Rollie, leading Marty out the front door of the store and into the dazzling sunshine. Rollie, in boots, made a track across the road to the schoolhouse and Marty, in sneakers, followed. Rollie, wearing leather mittens, shinnied up the flagpole and Marty followed him. Marty's hands were bare and the pole was icy cold. From the flagpole they were able to step onto the sloping roof and pull themselves up to the peak of the schoolhouse, where the belfry stood. The belfry had a false bottom, which Rollie removed.

"Look," said Rollie.

Marty peered down into the attic above the classroom.

"Follow me," said Rollie, and he dropped through the hole into the attic.

Marty dropped down beside him. It seemed even colder in this dark attic than it had outside. Marty blew on his fingers.

Rollie opened a small trapdoor.

"Look," he said.

Marty looked down into the classroom, strangely unfamiliar from this angle. The trapdoor was directly over the middle row of desks.

"Now as you drop down there, you have to swing yourself a little to the left or right so you land in an aisle. You don't want to land on a desk and break your leg."

Rollie let himself down through the opening, hung for a moment by his fingers, then swung to the left and landed neatly between two rows of desks.

Marty was afraid to jump. It was a long way down. He wanted to climb out on the roof and go back to the store, where it was warm. He looked up at the belfry hole, which was out of reach. He looked about him for something to stand on.

"What are you waiting for?" called Rollie.

There was nothing to stand on. The attic was empty.

"Come on. Are you yellow?"

Marty looked down. He remembered the time he had fallen off the roof of the shed at home and how he had bragged about it afterward, claiming that he had jumped on purpose. It was a drop from about this same height. But this was different. Here if he didn't land just right he would smash up a desk.

"Are you chicken to jump?" Rollie's words made steam in the cold classroom.

Marty let himself down through the hole, hung for a moment as Rollie had done, then dropped in a smooth arc and landed safely in the aisle.

"See?" said Rollie. "Nothing to it."

Marty nodded, his face cramped in a tight grin—an expression mostly of pride but partly of pain, for his feet and ankles stung from hitting the floor so hard.

"Now we light a fire," said Rollie. "Then we smoke and eat candy bars."

In the pile of split wood behind the potbellied stove Rollie looked for kindling but found none. "Those chunks are too big," he said. "To start a fire we need kindling. And paper."

Marty stepped over to his desk and handed Rollie his geography book.

"Not your own, dummy. Burn somebody else's."

Marty put his book back in his desk and took a reader from a desk in the front row.

"Whose is that?"

"My sister's."

"Are you sure you want to burn your sister's?"

Marty answered by tearing out a few pages and handing them to Rollie, who set them afire and dropped them into the stove. One by one, Marty added pages to the fire, then the cover of the reader, then a stick of wood. Then the fire went out.

It took five books to get a roaring fire started, four of Candy's and one of the teacher's. They added split wood. They sat on a bench close to the stove, eating and shivering. When their candy bars were gone, they lit cigarettes and chain-smoked for twenty minutes until their tongues burned and their eyes watered. Then as the classroom was beginning to get warm, they stood up to leave.

Marty was sick, but he didn't tell Rollie. He went to the door and tried to open it.

"Not that way," said Rollie. "It's locked. Here, follow me." He raised a window and climbed outside. Marty followed. The sun on the snow gave him a piercing headache. He struggled through the deep drifts toward the road as Rollie closed the window.

"Wait," said Rollie. "We have to go back up on the roof."

"We do?" Marty was dizzy.

"Of course, dummy. We have to close the trapdoor and the belfry hole so nobody knows we snuck in."

Marty vomited into the snow.

Vomiting was childish and Rollie chose to ignore it. He said, "If we leave the trapdoor open and the belfry hole open, we'll spoil it for the next time. You've always got to cover your tracks on jobs like this."

Marty raised his watery eyes to the roof and wondered where he would get the strength to climb the pole once more.

"Won't your ma and dad see us up there?" he asked, hoping.

"Their windows are all frosted."

"Can't you do it without me?" His teeth chattered.

"It takes two. One to drop into the attic to close the trapdoor and the other to pull him back up on the roof."

So up they went, Marty needing to be boosted up the pole

and up the sloping roof. They closed the trapdoor, and they replaced the platform at the base of the belfry. On the way down the pole, Marty's grip weakened and he plummeted into a snowdrift. He dragged himself across the road and through the store and into the house, where Candy and the Roosters were sitting down to breakfast. Rollie joined them, but Marty—his head pounding and his stomach churning—climbed the stairs and fell into bed. His sleep was fitful, and full of nightmares.

Chapter 5

Jemmy awoke in a canopy bed. She sat up and discovered herself in a flannel nightgown. The bedroom was large and colorful and full of sunshine. Tiny lavender flowers bloomed in the yellow wallpaper.

She crossed the room and looked out the window. Below her in the yard the man with the black beard was shoveling a path from the house to the barn. He stopped and rested, leaning on his shovel, and his breath steamed from his mouth in quick puffs. He looked up and saw Jemmy at the window. He raised his arm in a stiff wave.

Jemmy's clothes had dried overnight and had been laid out for her on a chair. She dressed, found her way downstairs, and edged into the kitchen, where she found the woman standing at the stove, her back to the doorway. She wore brown corduroy slacks and a brown turtleneck sweater, and her hair, which was nearly as dark as Jemmy's, was cut very short.

Jemmy said, "Hi."

"Oh, good morning, Jenny." The woman turned and smiled, a wooden spoon in one hand and a potholder in the other. "You're just in time to help me with breakfast. According to the radio, we'll be snowbound for most of the day, so we'll just have to make the best of it. I'll put you in charge of the toast, Jenny."

"It's Jemmy."

"Pardon me?"

"My name is Jemmy, not Jenny."

"Jemmy? That's an unusual name." She handed Jemmy a breadknife. "I suppose it's Indian."

"No, it's short for Gemstone."

"Gemstone? That's unusual too. But I like it. It suggests riches. We're the Chapmans. My name is Ann and my husband is Otis. Now here's a loaf of bread to slice, and over there is the toaster. We're having oatmeal and eggs and toast. Will you eat one egg or two?"

"I guess two." Jemmy set the loaf on the breadboard and began to cut.

"Of course two. All you've had since your ordeal was part of a bowl of stew. How are your cheeks? They still look flushed."

Jemmy put her hand to her face. "They feel kind of hot, but they're okay."

"Are they painful?" The woman touched Jemmy's cheek.

"No, not painful. Just kind of hot. And stiff."

"Yes, they feel feverish all right. I wonder if that's good or bad. I've never seen frostbite before."

"You haven't? You must be new around here." Jemmy was having trouble slicing the bread. It was very coarse and it crumbled as she tried to cut it.

"You're right. We moved here only last July. We came from Chicago. My husband is an artist, you see, and he's here to make studies of the land and the people. We bought this farmhouse and did it over from top to bottom, thinking we might make it our permanent home. Otis and I have been city people all our lives, and we thought a change in life style would be interesting. . . . Don't bear down so hard on the knife, Jemmy. You've got to saw back and forth. See here, like this. Thicker slices, and saw back and forth. You haven't sliced bread before, I guess."

"We always buy sliced."

"I'll give you my recipe for this cracked wheat. It's better for you."

Jemmy succeeded with the bread, and as she put two slices into the toaster she said, "I've never met an artist before."

"Otis is a painter and murals are his specialty. Quite often a city will commission him to paint a mural in a public building—usually something to do with the history of the area—and that's what he's preparing for now. He's been commissioned to paint a large mural in Minneapolis. It will cover one entire wall of the Tower Courtyard. Are you familiar with Minneapolis, Jemmy?"

"I was there once when I was little. I was in Reservation School at the time—about the fourth grade—and we all went down on a bus. We went to St. Paul to see the capitol and then to Minneapolis to see an art museum and a few other things. I think we stopped at about eight places in all."

"What impressed you the most?"

"A Burger King. I remember I was real hungry."

Ann Chapman laughed, and so did Jemmy.

"Well, that long ago you wouldn't have seen the Tower," said Ann. "It's the new skyscraper in downtown Minneapolis. At ground level it has a huge courtyard that covers nearly a city block. It's called the Tower Courtyard and it has indoor gardens and a fountain and shops and restaurants. It's covered by a glass dome, so it's bright and airy, like being outside. And on the south wall of the Courtyard is a space nearly a hundred feet long and forty feet high, which will be covered by Otis's mural. Most of the Tower is already occupied—offices mostly—and many of the shops in the Courtyard are open for business, but the official dedication won't take place until the mural is finished. Otis will start painting the day after New Year's and he's expected to finish by April first."

43

Ann Chapman stepped from the stove to the kitchen window and said quietly, as though to herself, "Look at all that snow."

Jemmy went and stood at her side. They looked out at the bearded man and the barn beyond him. When he stooped to lift a shovelful of snow, he was nearly hidden by the drift he was working in.

"Jemmy, have you read *Giants in the Earth?*"

"I don't remember. Is it science fiction?"

"No, it's about the pioneers who came to Minnesota and South Dakota and how they suffered, especially in the wintertime. One of the women, Per Hansa's wife, went crazy from too much snow. She lived in a sod house and there was nothing but snow and wilderness as far as she could see—like this—and she lost her mind."

Jemmy laughed a short, quick laugh. "This isn't wilderness. We're only about ten miles from Eagleton."

The woman turned to Jemmy, smiling. Her eyes were brown, her face pale and pretty. "I guess wilderness is relative. Compared to Chicago, this looks to me like the end of the earth. But don't get me wrong—it has a certain appeal. Late summer was lovely, and so was autumn—what there was of it. And I see the beauty in snow. Look at the graceful lines the wind has made. The drifts and hollows, like ocean waves frozen in place." She paused. "But there's something very lonely in all this snow, Jemmy. Not that I'm going to lose my mind over it; it's just that since yesterday's blizzard I think I can understand a little of what the pioneers felt when winter came."

"This snow won't last," said Jemmy. "Snow doesn't come to stay till the middle of November."

Ann returned to the stove, stirred the oatmeal, and said, "To tell the truth, Jemmy, there's even something lonely about Eagleton itself—those few square blocks of houses and stores huddled together, surrounded by forest. But I'm sure my opinion will change when I become better acquainted in Eagleton. How long will that take, do you think?"

"I hope it doesn't take you as long as it's taking me," said Jemmy, buttering toast. "I still don't feel at home in Eagleton."

"Really? But you've lived around here all your life. Certainly you have *some* friends in Eagleton."

"No. I've only got one friend. Sort of a friend. Her name is Roxanne Rooster, and she lives out on our road."

"But in high school, Jemmy. You have friends in your classes."

Jemmy stopped to think. She couldn't count Mr. Olson as a friend, at least not in the usual sense. "Not that I can think of," she said. She put more bread in the toaster.

"Is it because you're an Indian, Jemmy? Are they prejudiced against Indians in Eagleton?"

"No, not prejudiced." Jemmy spoke slowly, figuring out what she thought as she went along. "It's just that the Indians have never fit into Eagleton very well. I guess it depends what you want in life, and there isn't much in Eagleton that an Indian wants. I mean, there's a lot of country kids—white kids—who wish they lived in town so they could go out for sports after school. They've got girls' teams and boys' teams both. But Indian kids—at least the ones I know—would rather get up a game of softball behind Reservation School and make up their own rules and just have fun. That's their idea of a good time—playing softball when they feel like it and not playing when they don't feel like it—instead of doing everything on schedule. When you go out for school sports you do calisthenics every night all year and you only play a real game about once a week. It's that kind of thing—doing everything on schedule—that keeps Indians separate from whites, if you ask me."

Jemmy hadn't had this much to say for a long time, but Ann's questions had started her thinking. "Another thing is the way they look at you in Eagleton if you're an Indian.

45

I'm only half-Indian, but I get the same look. I wouldn't say it's a prejudiced look. It's what you'd call . . . I don't know . . . it isn't dislike exactly . . . it's more like pity. It's as if Indians made whites feel bad. And nobody likes to go around making other people feel bad. Like the high school principal. Every time he sees an Indian in the hall or in his office or somewhere, he gets this worried look on his face. It has to do with skipping and state-aid money and all that.

"Or being fat is another example. Roxanne Rooster's mother is real fat, and Roxanne can hardly stand to go into Eagleton with her because everybody always gives them a pitying look. Her mother gets the pitying look for being fat, and Roxanne gets it for having a fat mother. Now out on the reservation there's nothing wrong with being fat. If you want to be fat on the reservation, that's up to you."

"So you're happier on the reservation than you are in town," said Ann. She was breaking eggs into a cast-iron frying pan.

"No, not me. I don't belong on the reservation any more than I belong in Eagleton. I'm a half-breed."

"Really? I wouldn't have guessed that. You have what Otis would call the classic Indian face."

"I look like my mother. She was Chippewa."

"But surely half-breeds are welcome on the reservation."

"Oh, half-breeds can live there all right. There's nothing that says hundred-percent whites can't live there if they want to. But my dad never wanted to. We live two miles this side of the line. The school that my little brother and sister go to is right on the line."

The door opened and Otis Chapman came in, stomping snow off his boots and unwrapping a long scarf from around his neck.

"I got halfway to the barn and it was either quit shoveling or starve to death." He went directly to Jemmy and put his hand under her chin and studied her frostbite. Behind his full beard it was hard to read his expression. "Your face hurt?" he asked.

"No." She liked his hand under her chin. He was a big man with sure hands, and his voice was deep.

Ann asked him, "What about Socko? Do you think he's all right?"

"Socko's safe and sound in the barn. I'll have the path open by the time he gets hungry this afternoon, and he won't even know we had a blizzard." Otis took off his jacket and sat down and unlaced his boots.

"And the chickens?" said Ann. "Do you think the chickens lived through it?"

"I assume they had sense enough to go inside when it started snowing. It will take me a little longer to shovel over to the hen house, but I'm sure they're all snug in there. I heard the rooster crowing."

"The horse and chickens came with the farm," Ann explained to Jemmy. "We bought the place from an old couple who were retiring to a house in town, and they wouldn't sell unless we promised to take the horse and chickens."

"Socko's a good old nag," said Otis.

"Friendly as an overgrown dog," said Ann. "You see, Jemmy, having a horse and a few chickens lets us pretend we're farmers when we're really not. Our harvest consists of only two or three eggs a day."

"How many chickens?" asked Jemmy.

"Seven hens and a rooster."

"That's eight chicken dinners," said Jemmy.

Ann looked horrified. Otis said, "I'm afraid neither of us knows how to butcher a chicken; and besides, our chickens are more like pets than livestock. You ought to hear Ann out there at feeding time. She clucks with the hens."

"Otis, you lie." Ann laughed.

"See?" He pointed to his wife. "She's defensive about it, but I've heard her complaining about me to the chickens."

47

They sat down to breakfast. Otis and Jemmy ate hungrily while Ann nibbled. When they finished eating, they stayed at the table for a long time, sipping coffee and chatting. Being snowbound gave them a feeling of leisure, a lack of urgency. At first it was Ann who did most of the talking; she told of their buying the farm and hiring a carpenter to remodel the rooms and attending farm auctions to find sturdy old furniture like this round oak table in the kitchen. She said that she and Otis had built the kitchen fireplace themselves, using field stones. She spoke of Otis's work and recalled some of the famous people he had painted portraits of: senators, athletes, a bishop, an orchestra conductor. Jemmy hadn't heard of any of them.

Then the conversation shifted to Jemmy. "Now tell us about yourself," said Otis. "Tell us about school."

"Yes, and about your family," said Ann.

"We used to have chickens," said Jemmy, sidestepping the subjects of school and family. "Every spring my mother would order two dozen chickens and they would come in the mail."

"Chickens in the mail?" said Ann. She drew a piece of needlepoint onto her lap and began to stitch.

Jemmy nodded. "The chicks were three days old when they were mailed from Minneapolis and they were four days old when they were delivered. The mailman would drive into the yard and bring them up to the house so they wouldn't get cold. They were in long, flat boxes, with holes in the sides for breathing. You could hear them peeping."

"So you're an old hand at raising chickens," said Otis.

"That was a long time ago. But if I had to butcher one I think I could still do it. We quit having chickens when my mother died. Dad says chickens are a nuisance."

Ann said, "When did your mother die?"

"She died when Candy was born, and Candy is six." Jemmy was on her fourth cup of coffee and feeling a bit high-strung.

48

"Do you think of your mother often?"

"I think of her every day. Like yesterday when I came to the place in the woods where she and I used to pick blueberries." As Jemmy spoke she glanced from Ann to Otis. Otis's eyes were not as easy to look into as Ann's. His beard grew high on his cheeks and he seemed to be peering out from behind a disguise. "My mother and I only went berry picking once a year, but it's one of my best memories." She went on to describe what it was like to work up a sweat picking berries in the dark heat of the pine forest and to eat (from thirst as much as from hunger) more berries than were good for you. Then she described harvesting wild rice on the Turtle Egg River, her mother paddling and holding the canoe out of the current while Jemmy bent the stems of rice over the side of the canoe and flailed at them—the rice building up around her knees until, after a time, the canoe was heavy with rice and rode low in the water. She told how her mother sprinkled water on the rice before they put it into bags so that it would weigh more when they sold it to the rice buyer in Eagleton.

Otis put his elbows on the table where his plate had been and held his chin in his hands and gazed at Jemmy with an intensity that alarmed her. She felt herself flush.

"But anyhow, my mother's dead now and that's that."

Ann stitched and Otis stared. There was an awkward silence, and Jemmy, to break it, added, "I mean there's nothing can be done about her dying, is there? Just like nothing can be done about my dad's drinking."

Ann looked up from her needlepoint. "Your father drinks?"

Jemmy nodded.

"Is he a serious drinker? Does it interfere with his work?"

"He doesn't work at all anymore. I remember when he used to go to work every day. He painted houses. That was when my mother was still around. And even a couple of years ago he worked part time for a housepainter in Eagleton. But he had an accident one day and he hasn't worked since. He was up on a ladder in front of the Eagleton Theater—he was painting the marquee—and the ladder slipped and he fell on an old lady who was walking underneath. The old lady was crippled after that. And Dad never worked again."

Otis Chapman's eyes were still upon her. Why was he staring? What was he thinking?

"What about his disposition?" asked Ann. "Is he hard to live with?"

What could Jemmy say about her father's disposition? How could she convey the gloom that usually pervaded the house when her father was home? She said, "Most of the time he acts like he hates the world."

"Oh dear, that's no way to live," said Ann. "What about your brother and sister? Tell us about them."

"Marty's eleven, and he's a troublemaker. I'm not sure how much longer I can handle him. I think it's because Candy is my dad's pet, and Marty feels sort of left out. Candy's six. She gets A's in first grade. She's a little high and mighty sometimes, because she knows she's the only one of us that Dad cares much for, but you can't blame her for that."

Otis's eyes were on her again, probing her face so intensely that she stopped talking.

"Jemmy," he said, "what do you know about the Maiden of Eagle Rock?"

"The Maiden of Eagle Rock?" She shrugged. "She was the Chippewa that killed herself, wasn't she?"

"That's right. And what else do you know about her?"

"Not much. Her story was in our history books when we were sophomores, but our teacher said we shouldn't pay any attention to it. She said it wasn't true. It was only a legend."

"Only a legend! My God, Jemmy, your teacher must

have been an ignoramus. For certain periods of history legends are all we have to go by."

"She said there wasn't any proof."

"That's ridiculous. You don't need proof to believe in the Maiden of Eagle Rock. What's so unbelievable about a Chippewa girl falling in love with a Sioux brave? They belonged to enemy tribes, and therefore they couldn't marry. Is that unbelievable? And is it unbelievable that the Maiden committed suicide rather than live with a broken heart?"

Jemmy considered his questions. "I'd never kill myself over a man," she said.

Otis made a noise like a chuckle, but there was no sign of humor in his face. "Let me tell you the story, Jemmy. The Maiden leaped from Eagle Rock into the Turtle Egg River. You know the place, don't you? It's the cliff a mile or two this side of Eagleton."

"I know." She had stood at the top of Eagle Rock yesterday, in the snow.

"The Indians called the cliff Eagle Rock because eagles nested there. And they still do—I've seen them."

"So have I."

"Yes, well, it's a drop of about a hundred and forty feet from the top of the rock to the river. I've been doing a lot of sketching there because the Maiden of Eagle Rock is the subject of a mural I've been commissioned to paint in Minneapolis. And as I've been sketching I've thought a lot about the story, Jemmy. How the Maiden met the brave, and so forth. And now as I listen to you tell about berry picking, I see how it might have been. Let's imagine it like this. Let's say there was a lull in the fighting between the Sioux and the Chippewa. After all, they couldn't have been at each other's throats every day of the year. They had other business. They had to have time to hunt. They had to catch fish. They had to pick berries. So let's say the blueberries were ripe, Jemmy, and this Chippewa girl went into the forest with her mother, the way you used to do. And there in the forest she met this Sioux brave. He was out stalking deer, let's say. The Maiden had moved off some distance from her mother, and there was the brave, following her. They kissed. They fell in love. They made plans to meet again. And long after the berries were gone, they kept meeting in the forest, but of course they couldn't bring their love out into the light. They had to keep it in the shadows of the forest because their people were enemies. Then came the showdown. In the fall of 1858 the final battle was fought between the two tribes for control of Eagle Rock. The brave lined up with his people. His loyalty to his tribe was stronger than his love for the Maiden. His side lost, and after the battle the Maiden never saw him again. She leaped from Eagle Rock and landed on the boulders along the river—dead instantly. I've spent so much time out there, Jemmy, I feel I can show you the exact spot where she died."

"What happened to the brave?" Legend or not, Jemmy was caught up in the story.

"Who knows? That part of the tale hasn't come down to us. After the battle, the Sioux moved west and settled in the Dakotas. Nobody knows if the brave went with them or if he died in the battle. You have to imagine that part for yourself."

Jemmy imagined that he survived.

Ann was at the sink, getting ready to wash dishes. "Why don't you tell her what this is all leading up to, Otis? I can read your mind."

Otis didn't seem to hear. He was gazing at Jemmy.

"I can read your mind, Otis. You've found the face you've been looking for, haven't you?"

Otis leaned back in his chair and crossed his arms. "Jemmy, I want you to be the Maiden of Eagle Rock."

Jemmy was puzzled.

"You see, the most prominent part of my mural will be the Maiden. She will be in the foreground, looking directly at the viewer. In the distance will be Eagle Rock itself, rising over the river. It's a very dramatic landscape and it will make a nice backdrop. And in the middle ground we'll see the Sioux brave, retreating. He will be walking away, into the picture, but he will be looking back over his shoulder at the Maiden. He is leaving, but his heart is lingering behind. And front and center—and forty feet high—will be the Maiden, looking out at the viewer. All my preliminary work is done except my studies of the Maiden, Jemmy. I want you to be the Maiden."

Jemmy looked away.

"What do you say? Will you?"

She nodded. "If you think I'll do." She couldn't quite believe that she would do, for the Maiden was said to be very beautiful.

"Splendid. We'll work here in my studio. When can you come for your first sitting?"

She could come tomorrow, Thursday, but she didn't want to admit that she had quit school. "I can come on Saturday," she said.

"Splendid."

In midafternoon the county plow opened the road past the Chapmans' farm, and a short time later a man with a snowplow attached to his truck drove out from Eagleton (Otis had summoned him by phone) and cleared the driveway. He also made a path to the hen house and he finished the path to the barn that Otis had started. Before he left, he dropped off a five-gallon can of gasoline for Jemmy's car.

Jemmy went to the barn and fed Socko while Ann carried a pan of feed to the hungry chickens. Then Jemmy and Ann and Otis got into the Chapmans' car—a tiny new car the color of a carrot—and Otis drove through the forest and past the stone foundation and past the house with the *Mean Dog* sign. They found Jemmy's car half buried in the snow thrown up by the plow. They dug it out and poured the five gallons of gasoline into the tank. By pumping the accelerator and crossing her fingers, Jemmy got the engine started. Otis and Ann pushed from behind while Jemmy spun the wheels, and the car slowly moved clear.

Jemmy shifted into neutral, got out, and said, "Thank you for everything. I'll pay you for the gas when I get money from Dad."

"Don't worry about it," said Otis. "Just be sure to show up on Saturday morning so we can get started on your portrait. No later than ten o'clock."

"Come earlier," said Ann. "We'll have breakfast." She put her arm around Jemmy's shoulders and smiled and gave her a little squeeze.

Jemmy drove home feeling light-headed, as though she had spent the last twenty-four hours in a high and rarified atmosphere, as though she had caught a glimpse of life on an alien—and better—planet.

But the sight of her father brought her suddenly down to earth. As she drew near home, she saw him making his way through the deep snow of their driveway. When she slowed to a stop at the side of the plowed road, he came over to the car with something like frenzy in his eyes. He wore three or four sweaters and a stocking cap. He had run out of vodka early in the day and now he had the shakes. Jemmy got out from behind the wheel and her father got in. Without a word of greeting or explanation, he pulled the door shut and sped away to Stan Rooster's lifesaving supply of liquor.

Marty and Candy were already home, having been delivered by Roxanne Rooster. In the kitchen, Candy hugged Jemmy around the legs. Marty, too, was glad to see her, but he didn't believe in hugging. Jemmy bent down and squeezed Candy tightly around the shoulders, imitating Ann Chapman's hug, then she caught Marty and did the same to him, though he fought it. Then she went into her bedroom and hid the sack containing Candy's new jeans in the closet.

She would not give them to her until she had a new pair for Marty as well.

The house was chilly. Jemmy turned up the oil burner in the front room. She went outside, brushed snow off the woodpile, and brought in half a dozen sticks of oak to start a fire in the kitchen range. She cooked a pot of chili, and at supper she tried to make conversation with Marty and Candy. She wanted this kitchen table to be like the Chapmans' table, a place for talk, but it didn't work. Marty and Candy, famished, ate with their noses in their bowls.

"How did you like staying with the Roosters?" Jemmy asked them.

"I slept with Roxanne," said Candy. "She's got four lipsticks."

"And what about you, Marty? Did you sleep with Rollie?"

"Yeah."

"And she's got perfume," said Candy.

"Were you good at the Roosters'?"

Candy nodded, solemnly.

"And was Marty good?"

Candy frowned. "Not very."

That night, long after Candy had fallen asleep at her side, Jemmy lay awake thinking about the Chapmans, their bright kitchen, the warmth of their stone fireplace, the warmth of their talk, the soft canopy bed she had slept in. What would Candy say if she could see that bed? Compared to this worn-out spring and mattress, it was hardly recognizable as a bed. This spring and mattress had originally been their mother and father's bed, but when their mother died everybody switched places. Because the crib was in this room, Stott—to get away from the noisy baby—had moved to Marty's narrow bed in the room with no window. Marty had moved to the living room couch, which had been Jemmy's bed, and Jemmy had moved into this room with the crib. Jemmy was eleven at the time, and with the help of Mrs. Rooster and another woman from the reservation, a cousin of her mother's, she took care of the new baby. Jemmy missed a lot of school in those years, attending only when her father stayed home from work or the cousin from the reservation agreed to spend the day, or, as happened quite often, the baby was left with the Roosters. One night when Candy was three she left her crib and climbed in with Jemmy, and they had been sharing this spring and mattress ever since.

Through the bedroom window, Jemmy saw the moon rising over the forest. It was orange and very large. It seemed to be only about three miles away and hanging over the Chapmans' farm. She stared at the moon and wondered about the Chapmans. If she let herself become fond of them, would they prove steadfast, or would they disappoint her? From Roxanne and her classmates in Eagleton, and especially from her father, Jemmy had learned to keep her distance from people, to be self-sufficient, to be wary of affection. Keeping your distance was the safest way. You wouldn't get hurt so easily. She had been close to her mother, and her mother had died.

Jemmy sat up in bed and lit a cigarette. What would it be like to go to Minneapolis and see yourself on a wall forty feet high? She was determined to go. One way or another, as soon as the mural was finished, she would go. It was 205 miles to Minneapolis. If her father wouldn't let her take the Dodge, she would ride a bus. She would take Marty and Candy along and they would eat in a restaurant.

Jemmy coughed, and Candy stirred in her sleep. Jemmy wondered what it would feel like to stand before the mural and have people notice the resemblance. Would that be embarrassing or exciting? Probably both. If asked, would she admit that she had been the model? Yes. She would tell them the story of the Maiden. The Maiden was unlucky in love, she would tell them. But the Maiden was stupid to kill herself, she would add.

Jemmy looked at the moon, which was higher now, and paler. How pleased her mother would have been to see Jemmy in the mural, representing Minnesota's Chippewa heritage. Her mother has been proud of her Indian blood, and she insisted that Jemmy be the same. But it was hard to be proud of it when you went to school in Eagleton. If you were an Indian in Eagleton it was hard to make friends and feel comfortable. Jemmy had spent the last three years feeling slightly ashamed of her Indianness. What was it her mother used to say? "There are cycles in our lives like the cycles of the seasons." Her mother used to say that not only did the natural world change as time went by, people changed too. Their moods changed, and so did their attitudes and their luck. And now Jemmy felt it happening to herself. After three years of being slightly ashamed of her Indian ancestry, she found herself singled out because of it. For the first time in years, Jemmy was glad to be Indian.

She put out the cigarette and pulled the covers up to her chin. What was it like to sit for a portrait? How long did you have to be perfectly still? Were you permitted to blink? Why, of all Indian girls around Eagleton, had Otis chosen her? Had he really chosen her, she wondered drowsily, or was it a dream?

She slept.

Chapter 6

On Saturday morning Jemmy put on her best clothes— her least-worn pair of jeans and the shirt her father had given her for Christmas last year. It was a man's red flannel shirt from the Heap Big Discount Store.

She woke up Marty and Candy and gave them breakfast. Her father was still asleep.

"For lunch you can make sandwiches for yourselves," she told Marty and Candy as they ate. "I'll be home later this afternoon."

"Where are you going?" asked Candy.

"Take us along," said Marty.

"Never mind, I have an appointment. I'll see you at suppertime."

"What's wrong with your face?" asked Candy.

"Yeah, it looks weird," said Marty.

"It's peeling. I froze it in the blizzard. Now keep the house neat. It it's a mess when I get home, I'll make you clean it up."

Outside it was warm. The road was soft mud. Snowbanks were melting into pools. The few robins and blackbirds that had not yet flown south were perched on barbed-wire fences, sunning themselves and preening.

Jemmy was pleased to be leaving the house for a few hours. Her father was gloomy most of the time and Marty was in trouble at school. Her father used to have ups as well as downs, but lately, it seemed to Jemmy, he was always down. As for Marty, his teacher Miss Frost had come to see Jemmy on Thursday; she said that Marty and Rollie Rooster had broken into and vandalized the schoolhouse on the morning after the blizzard. Their tracks in the snow gave them away. As punishment they were going to have to remain after school each day for the rest of October and for most of November, and Jemmy was expected to help supervise them. If Marty was already a problem in the fifth grade, how could Jemmy expect to control him in years to come?

Well, she would worry about that some other day. She didn't want to spoil her breakfast with the Chapmans by brooding over her troubles. How nice to be invited out for breakfast. The last invitation Jemmy could remember was to Roxanne Rooster's eleventh birthday party. That was six years ago. Several times this week Jemmy had been tempted to go to Rooster's and tell Roxanne about the portrait, just for the sake of watching her turn green. But she overcame the urge, recalling what her mother used to say about being kind, even to people you didn't like very much.

She drove up the sloping driveway into the Chapmans' yard and parked under the big tree. In the pasture near the barn the old horse was grazing on a patch of wet grass between snowbanks. Jemmy called, "Hi, Socko," and he raised his head. He looked at her for a moment, then resumed eating. She went to the house and knocked on the kitchen door.

"My goodness, Jemmy, what's the matter with your face?" said Ann, obviously shocked at her appearance.

"It isn't *that* bad, is it?" said Jemmy, stepping inside.

Ann put forward a tentative hand to touch her cheek.

"It's just peeling," said Jemmy. "It's nothing to get excited about."

"But it looks so painful!"

"It doesn't hurt. It's just sort of dry and scabby feeling."

"Otis, look here, at Jemmy's face. She's losing a layer of skin. I never saw anything like it."

Otis came into the kitchen from his studio and with his large hand under her chin he examined her face. "It's probably not serious," he said, "but if you want, we can take you into town to the doctor."

"Who needs a doctor? Peeling from frostbite is the same as peeling from sunburn. Nobody goes to a doctor for that."

Otis shrugged and Ann allowed herself to be reassured. She served breakfast. French toast and sausage. Orange juice and coffee. As before, they were reluctant to leave the table when they finished eating, and their conversation focused on Jemmy. How was her family? How was school?

"My family's okay," she said, then decided to level with the Chapmans. "I mean it's the same as usual. Dad's grumpy and Marty's in trouble. Candy's fine. She's too young to be a problem."

"What's Marty's trouble?"

"He broke into Reservation School. He and Rollie Rooster. They did it the morning after the blizzard, and the teacher could tell by the tracks in the snow who it was. So now the Reservation School Board has barred all the windows with a heavy screen so nobody can break in anymore." Once again, Jemmy found she could talk to the Chapmans with surprising ease. It was impossible not to like them.

"It sounds like the school board is overreacting," said Ann. She drew her needlepoint onto her lap.

"Not really. Besides break-ins, they've had a lot of problems with broken windows lately."

"So what did they do to Marty?" asked Otis.

"He and Rollie Rooster have to stay after school an hour a day till Thanksgiving and do janitor work. That's about five more weeks. They sweep the floor and wash the black-

60

board and bring in firewood and things like that. It serves them right. The only trouble is that the teacher, Miss Frost, can't stay after school every night, and she can't trust Marty and Rollie to be there alone, so twice a week I have to go and sit in the schoolroom for an hour while they do their work. But I guess I don't mind it too much. I draw when I'm there. They have drawing paper and those flat sketching pencils. I used to draw a lot when I was in the grades."

"What did you draw?" Otis asked.

"Trees. Fences. You know, stuff around here. I still do sometimes."

"Will you bring us some of your work? We'd like to see it."

"Oh, I hardly ever keep any of my drawings. Most of them aren't any good. I burn them in the kitchen range."

"Burn them!" said Ann. "Why on earth would you burn them?"

"Because there's usually something wrong with them. Something's crooked that ought to be straight—you know what I mean. Trees, for instance. I can never get trees the way I want them. In grade school the teacher said our trees should look as if birds could fly through them—you know, light and leafy. But my trees always look too solid. If a bird tried to fly through one of mine it would knock itself out."

Ann laughed. Otis nodded seriously, perhaps recalling trees of his own that might have caused concussions in birds.

"Once I drew an oak tree like the one by your driveway; I showed it to Roxanne Rooster on the school bus and she said it looked like a lollipop on a stick. That's when I decided never to show my drawing to anybody again."

"But you must show them to us," said Otis. "Ann and I have been going out on sketching trips. You can come with us."

Another invitation. Jemmy felt rich. "You mean *both* of you are artists?"

"Heavens no," said Ann.

"She's learning," said Otis. "You see, the reason she married me was so that she could get free art lessons."

Ann laughed; Otis did not. Jemmy wished Otis would loosen up his face and show what he was feeling, the way his wife did.

He said, "Now, as for you, Jemmy, bring your drawings next time and we'll look them over. I hope you're taking art in school. I've met the Eagleton art teacher and he strikes me as very good."

Jemmy looked Otis in the eye and blurted, "I don't go to school anymore. I quit last Tuesday, the day of the blizzard." Her words surprised her. Her instinct for telling the truth was stronger than her wish to conceal it, and the words had come out before she quite realized what she was saying. Ann dropped her needlepoint and Otis pursed his lips and frowned.

"Why?" Ann asked.

"Dad says." One good thing about following someone else's orders, you didn't have to explain. You simply repeated the order. "Dad says I have to help out at home, and high school wasn't getting me anyplace." This answer had satisfied the school nurse and the principal's secretary. Now she looked from Otis to Ann to see if it satisfied them. It seemed to. Or if it didn't satisfy them, at least it gave them pause. Ann was biting her lip and Otis had turned away.

After a moment Ann said, "Certainly you plan to go back someday and finish."

Jemmy shrugged.

"Everybody needs at least a high school diploma."

Jemmy nodded. So she had heard.

"Jemmy, do you think it was right to quit?" Otis asked.

"Dad says."

"But you, Jemmy. What do *you* say? What do *you* think?"

She looked into the fireplace, where a small flame danced. "I don't know," she said.

"How does quitting make you *feel*?" Otis prompted. "What are your feelings about it?"

"I never felt better."

Ann sighed. There was a movement in her shoulders—something like a shudder.

Otis looked at his watch and said, "It's ten, Jemmy. Come into my studio and we'll go to work. The light is best between ten and two. We'll talk about school another time."

The dining room of the Chapmans' farmhouse had been converted into a studio. The north wall was entirely glass, and when Otis pulled open the draperies the room was flooded with shadowless light.

Jemmy drew a comb from her purse, but Otis said, "No—I want your hair just as it is." He showed her to a chair ten feet from his easel and asked her to sit. "In the mural you'll be standing, but for now I want to concentrate on your face." Touching her gently on the temples, he moved her head to the precise angle he wished her to hold. "I want your eyes on me but your head turned slightly to the left, toward the light."

He then put on an apron, quickly mixed a pile of dark paint on his palette, and went immediately to work on a large rectangle of stretched canvas.

Jemmy was amazed at the size of the brush he used and at the recklessness of his strokes. He might have been painting a house. As he worked, his eyes were almost constantly on her face and only briefly on the canvas. At first she found it disconcerting—and flattering—to be looked at so closely and she could hardly resist raising her hand to straighten her hair, but soon she realized that he was not really paying much attention to her as a person; he saw her merely as a problem in painting, and although their eyes met again and again, his preoccupation with his art was a barrier to any communication. Somewhere Jemmy had read that eyes were the windows of the soul, but she decided it wasn't true in this case. Eyes, to the painter, were simply eyes.

Then suddenly, to her surprise, Otis threw down his brush and backed away from the canvas.

"It's no use," he said. "I can't paint you today. Your peeling skin is so distracting I can't concentrate on the painting."

Jemmy brought her hands up to her cheeks in embarrassment.

"I'm sorry, Jemmy, but I can't do anything more until your skin gets back to normal. It's so red and sore-looking that it pulls my eyes away from the shapes I should be seeing. It's a shame you made the trip for nothing. Can you come back next week?"

"Yes," she said, relieved not to be dismissed for good.

"Okay, so we'll close up shop for now." He picked up his brush and swished it around in a cup of turpentine.

Jemmy approached the canvas from behind. "Can I look?"

"Of course. But there isn't much to see, just the shapes— very bad strokes—the shadows under the eyebrows, the nose. See? What do you think?"

She was fascinated. All the lines were the same muddy color—a dark greenish brown—but they were true lines. They represented a face, and not only a face, an expression. She was seized by a desire to paint.

"Well?" he said.

"Do you think I could learn to paint?"

Otis took the canvas from the easel and replaced it with a new one, a smaller one. He picked a magazine off a table and tore out a page and taped it to the easel, above the canvas. It was a photo of Elizabeth Taylor.

"Let me demonstrate. See here. Dip your brush into this mixture of turpentine and linseed oil. Then dip it into this paint . . . You want the paint thin on your brush, like a

wash. Now see here, you attack the dark areas first
. . . like this . . . the shadow under the chin . . . the
dark side of her face . . . the shadow along her nose
. . . her dark hair. See? Like that." It took him less than a
minute to produce a sketch in paint so thin that it was
running in rivulets down the canvas.

He replaced the Elizabeth Taylor canvas with a new one,
and he put the brush in Jemmy's hand. He went to the
model's chair and settled himself into position, his eyes on
Jemmy, his face turned slightly toward the light.

"Go ahead," he said. "Paint."

"Are you serious?"

"Paint."

Jemmy labored awkwardly for several minutes, and when
Ann came into the studio with three cups of coffee on a tray
she was glad of the excuse to put down her brush.

"What's going on?" asked Ann. "The model painting a
picture of the artist?"

"It's no good," said Jemmy, backing away from her
work.

Otis examined the painting. He picked up a brush and a
rag and made several adjustments. He lowered an ear and
raised the hairline over the forehead.

"The basic shape of the head is fine," he said. "And the
shadows around the eyes are right. But here—you've got
my beard too large." With the rag he reduced the mass of
beard. "Now isn't that more like it?"

"No, your beard is bushier than that," said Jemmy.

"She's right," said Ann. "I think you tend to underesti-
mate how it dominates your face. Let her paint you the way
she sees you, Otis. It's her painting." There was a trace of
impatience in this last remark, and both Otis and Jemmy
looked at Ann in surprise.

"Here, have some coffee," she said. She set down the
tray and arranged a circle of chairs near the wall of
windows. They sat—Ann with her back to the view—and

sipped their coffee, then after a minute Ann got up and pulled the draperies nearly shut.

"This is not my favorite room," she explained to Jemmy. "These windows let in so much of the outside that I feel uncomfortable in here. Sort of exposed. The kitchen is much more snug, don't you think?"

"I like the kitchen," said Jemmy. She looked out through the opening in the curtains. Beyond the oak tree and the barn she could see the road stretching away into the woods. "But this is such a nice view," she added.

"Yes, I agree, but at the same time it seems too vast. Ever since the blizzard I haven't felt quite comfortable living so far from nowhere."

"Come January we'll be in Minneapolis for three months," said Otis. "You'll enjoy Minneapolis."

Ann nodded.

Jemmy finished her coffee and said she had to go to town for groceries.

"We'll all go and take our car," said Ann, her face brightening. "Any excuse to mingle with humanity."

They put on their jackets and went out to the carrot-colored car. Otis asked Ann to drive, and he got into the back seat with his sketchbook. Twice in the forest he asked Ann to stop for a minute so that he could sketch a stand of pines, and when they reached Eagle Rock he suggested they get out for a look at the river.

They left the car and walked to the edge of the precipice. Below them the river, narrow from this height, glinted like a mirror. Upstream in the valley were the rooftops of Eagleton, and downstream was the white water of a stony rapids. Jemmy looked straight down at the boulders far beneath her. There, where the Maiden had died a hundred and twenty years ago, two crows were hopping about, searching for food.

"Imagine jumping," said Ann, backing away. "It's too horrible."

Jemmy tried to imagine it and couldn't. How could you jump from a place this beautiful? The view alone was enough to make you forget your troubles.

Otis pointed across the river. "That's where I did most of my sketching. In the mural we'll be looking at this bluff from over there."

"Let's go," said Ann. "It's chilly."

"If we wait awhile, we might see an eagle," said Otis. "They nest below us in the face of the cliff."

They searched the sky and the valley for eagles, but saw none. The breeze at this height was cold, and after a minute Ann started for the car. Otis and Jemmy followed her.

In Eagleton Jemmy accompanied the Chapmans into shops she had never entered before. They looked at dresses, at antiques, and at paperback books. In the jewelry store they examined a display of necklaces, and the Chapmans asked Jemmy which one she liked best.

It was hard to decide. The jeweler came forward with his eyepiece attached to his forehead like a third eye. He looked from the Chapmans to Jemmy and back again. Who were these strangers, he wondered, and why were they associating with an Indian dressed in frayed clothes that didn't fit?

Jemmy pointed to a necklace resembling one that Roxanne Rooster wore—a small turquoise stone on a silver chain.

The jeweler removed it from the display and handed it to Ann. Ann put it around Jemmy's neck. The jeweler's eyebrows—and with them his extra eye—lifted in amazement.

"For me?" said Jemmy.

"For you," said Ann.

"For you," said Otis, paying for it. Eight ninety-five.

"But it isn't even Christmas or anything," said Jemmy.

Ann gave her a little squeeze around the shoulders, and the jeweler stared after them as they left the store.

Next they went into a shoe store, and while Ann tried on

boots Jemmy went to a mirror and studied the blue stone at her throat.

Then they split up. Otis went one direction for chicken feed and Ann went another for library books. With her father's welfare check, Jemmy bought groceries at Gene's Market, then cigarettes and a pair of jeans for Marty at the Heap Big Discount Store.

At the appointed time Jemmy went into Eagleton Eatery for lunch. She saw that the Chapmans had not yet arrived, and carrying her two large bags of groceries and feeling self-conscious, she walked over to a table and sat down. She set the groceries on the floor beside her chair.

"Hey, Jemmy."

She looked toward the back of the restaurant and saw Roxanne Rooster in a booth with Morrie Benjamin.

"Hi," Jemmy said, waving.

"Come on back," called Roxanne.

Jemmy hesitated. Morrie was such a creep. She looked about her at the other tables, where everyone seemed to be watching her. She picked up her groceries and went to the booth. The company of creeps was preferable to the stares of strangers.

Morrie said, "What are you doing here?" and Roxanne said, "Where did you get that necklace?" Neither of them moved over to make room for Jemmy to sit. On the table between them were empty Coke glasses and a full ashtray.

"I'm here with friends," said Jemmy. She stood awkwardly at the booth, holding her groceries. She saw with satisfaction that Roxanne had the beginnings of a large new pimple on her chin.

"Let's see what's in your purse today," said Morrie. He lifted the flap of the fringed leather purse that hung from Jemmy's shoulder. She set her groceries on the table and slapped his hand. He hooted, pretending pain.

"Is that my necklace?" said Roxanne, peering closely at Jemmy's throat.

"Let's see what's in these bags," said Morrie, examining her groceries.

"That's my necklace, Jemmy. Did Candy take that home from my place the other night?"

"Look here," said Morrie. "She's got four rolls of toilet paper."

"Because if that's my necklace, Jemmy, you just better hand it over."

Jemmy picked up her groceries and said, "This necklace was given to me by those people over there—that man and woman coming in the door."

Roxanne and Morrie turned to look.

"Their name is Chapman. He's Otis Chapman the artist, and that's his wife Ann. They live out on the road past Eagle Rock. They're friends of mine."

"You expect us to believe that?" said Morrie.

"And that isn't all. Otis is using me as the model for his big mural in Minneapolis. I'm going to be the Maiden of Eagle Rock. It's going to be in the Tower Courtyard and they're paying him thousands of dollars to paint it."

Roxanne squinted through her false eyelashes. "Are you kidding?"

"You're dreaming," said Morrie.

Jemmy walked away without another word.

After lunch Otis drove home with Ann at his side, reading a book, and Jemmy riding in the back seat. They took the road that ran along the south side of the river—Jemmy's old school-bus route—and when they reached the point opposite Eagle Rock, Otis stopped the car.

Ann looked up from her book. "What's wrong?"

"Nothing," said Otis. "It's time to sketch." From a sack of things he had bought in town, he drew out a new sketchbook and a pencil and handed them over the seat to Jemmy.

"These are yours," he said, "and there's no better place

to break in a sketchbook than right here. Step outside a minute, and I'll get you started on a drawing of Eagle Rock."

Jemmy and Otis got out. Ann resumed reading.

"I spent days going up and down this road making sketches of the Rock," said Otis. "Come along, I'll show you the angle I finally settled on."

Jemmy followed him down the road. The sun had grown pale behind a film of high, thin clouds, and she buttoned her jacket against the cold breeze off the river.

"Right here," said Otis, planting himself on the shoulder of the road and looking across the water. He put his hands up in front of his face, palms outward, as though pressing them against a window, and he brought the tips of his thumbs together in front of his nose, thus producing a frame—or at least the bottom and sides of a frame—through which he viewed the scene.

"See how this clump of birch trees in the foreground balances the cliff in the background. Here, Jemmy, make a frame out of your hands like this. It helps you compose the picture. It helps you imagine how it will look when it's finished."

She handed him her sketchbook and pencil, and she made a frame out of her hands.

"That's neat," she said. She turned in several directions, looking through the frame. "Neat," she said again, fascinated to learn that by this simple trick of the hands you could make an instant picture of anything you looked at.

Otis opened the sketchbook to the first page and handed it to her. "Cradle it in your left arm," he said. He took a jackknife from his pocket and put a point on the new drawing pencil. "Here, now you're ready to draw."

Jemmy stood at the edge of the road, strands of her long hair lifting and dropping in the breeze, and she drew a line representing the far shore of the river. She felt more confident with pencil and paper than she had with brush and canvas. High above the horizontal line she drew the rocky crest of the cliff. Next, with quick strokes, she drew the trunks of the birch trees in the foreground.

Then she saw an eagle. Otis saw it too, and they both said "Look!" at the same instant. Halfway up the face of the cliff a golden eagle had sprung out from a ledge and was soaring overhead, circling over the river in a slow graceful curve, riding the wind, turning and dipping and rising with scarcely a flap of his broad wings.

"A golden eagle," said Otis. "See his golden head."

"Yes," said Jemmy, absorbed in the beauty of his sweeping flight. With each circle he let the wind carry him farther and farther down the river until he was a speck floating out of sight.

"What a performance," said Otis.

Jemmy was speechless, for as the eagle disappeared she felt a sharp pang of loss, an emotion so sudden and deep that it took her breath away, as though the eagle had been sent as a sign—as though the circles he traced in the sky were the words of a message she couldn't decipher but a message meant for her alone. She didn't know why, but for a moment she felt very close to her mother.

"Beautiful," Otis murmured at her side.

When they reached the farm Jemmy transferred her groceries from the Chapmans' car to the Dodge. She thanked them again for the necklace and the lunch.

"We'll expect you on Monday," said Otis.

"What if my face is still peeling?"

"Come anyway," said Ann. "We'll visit. Or we'll go to town." Her smile looked genuinely happy, and Jemmy saw no trace of her earlier discontent.

On her way home, Jemmy stopped the Dodge to look down a narrow side road that climbed a wooded hillside. She held her hands up in the shape of a frame and imagined the scene as a drawing. How exciting to be an artist, she thought, and to see the world as a vast collection of potential paintings.

Farther on, a quarter of a mile from home, she stopped once more and framed her house and shed, trying to see them as a painting, but it didn't work. There was nothing picturesque about the Stott place. The house and shed were too squat and crooked to be artistic, and they were dwarfed by the tall pine forest in the background. This was the first time she had ever taken an objective look at her home, and she felt an unfamiliar twinge of uneasiness, something bordering on fear. This was where problems awaited her— Marty's wild behavior and her father's dark moods. Moreover, viewing her home now as an artist might, she saw the remoteness that Ann objected to. Now, as never before, Jemmy was conscious of how far the Stotts lived from the rest of humanity, conscious of how her only neighbors were the deep forest and the flat empty fields.

Chapter 7

On Monday morning Jemmy's face was all but healed. She delivered Marty and Candy to Reservation School, then she drove to the Chapmans', where after breakfast Otis resumed work on her portrait.

Later in the morning, long after his family had left the house, Stott rose from his bed and found that he was out of cigarettes. He dressed and stepped outside, intending to drive to Rooster's Store, but the Dodge was gone. Standing on the doorstep, he clenched his fists and cursed.

In Eagleton, shortly before noon, Roxanne Rooster excused herself from study hall. She went to the washroom and applied a fresh coat of eye shadow and powdered the pimple on her chin, then she went to the office and asked to see the principal.

The secretary was reading a section of the *Minneapolis Tribune*, and without looking up she said, "Go ahead in."

Roxanne stepped through the door of the inner office.

"Yes?" said the gray-faced principal, looking up from another section of the *Tribune*.

"I'm Roxanne Rooster from the reservation, and I'd like to tell you something that's happening, and I wonder what you think of it." She drew apart her long hair and hooked it

73

over her ears so that the principal could appreciate the beauty of her eyes.

"Sit down," he said, closing the newspaper.

"Do you remember Jemmy Stott?"

"Jemmy Stott? No, the name doesn't ring a bell."

"She was a senior until last week. She dropped out."

The principal shook his head grimly.

"Now me, I'd never think of dropping out. So far this year I haven't missed a day of school."

The principal's face brightened slightly, but not as much as Roxanne had hoped. Perhaps she was coming on too strong, was acting too egotistical for the principal's taste. Or, on the other hand, maybe he needed more evidence concerning her scholarship. She decided to risk a little more bragging.

"I've got A's going in English and gym, and B's in the rest."

"That's very good," said the principal. "Now please come to the point."

"The point is—have you ever heard of Otis Chapman?"

"Otis Chapman, the famous painter. I've met him personally. We're honored to have him living in our area."

"Well, he's going to be painting this gigantic picture down in Minneapolis. It's all about the Maiden of Eagle Rock, and he wants Jemmy Stott to be his model for the Maiden, and I'm wondering if you think that's fair."

"What would be unfair about it?"

"What I mean is, we're told that the only way we'll succeed in life is if we stay in school and get our diplomas, but now Jemmy, a dropout, gets to be the Maiden of Eagle Rock. And besides, she isn't even all Indian. She's only half."

The principal was silent for a few moments, formulating his reply. He saw the logic in what she was saying, but he also saw her self-serving motives.

"Choosing a model is the artist's privilege," he said.

"Well, yes, I suppose that's true." The principal's attitude disappointed Roxanne, and she considered giving up. However, having come this far, she pressed onward. "I wonder if it might set a bad example for the younger kids when somebody like Jemmy is honored like this. Just think how it would be if some Indian from the senior class—some full-blooded Chippewa who never misses school—would be the model instead. I bet a lot of Indian kids would keep going till they graduated."

The principal's expression remained impassive, but his words seemed to hold out hope: "Your suggestion has a certain logic."

Roxanne nodded, smiling. "Maybe if you spoke to Mr. Chapman . . ."

The principal frowned. "Well, that would be quite presumptuous of me, I'm afraid. And even if Mr. Chapman did agree to change models, he wouldn't have many Indian girls to choose from in high school."

Roxanne beamed.

"It's a touchy question. I might talk to him, and I might not."

"I think he'll listen to reason," said Roxanne. "I saw him in the Eatery on Saturday. He looks like a reasonable man."

"I'll think it over." The principal opened the *Tribune*, his gesture of dismissal.

During noon hour, the principal brought up the subject at the faculty lunch table. He told Mr. Olson that some girl named Stott had been chosen, undeservedly, to be the Maiden. He said he might talk to Otis Chapman and try to change his mind. He saw no harm in at least calling him up and sounding him out.

Mr. Olson looked up from his fish sticks in disbelief.

"Being the Maiden is a big honor," said the principal. "It should go to an achiever, not to a dropout."

"An achiever?" said Mr. Olson. "What do you mean, an achiever?"

"I mean an academic achiever, someone with ambition enough to stay in school and make something of herself. Surely I don't need to define achievement for you."

"But I happen to know that Jemmy Stott quit school in order to take care of the younger kids in her family. Her father drinks and her mother is dead and Jemmy is holding the family together. That's my idea of achievement." Mr. Olson crumpled his paper napkin into a ball and dropped it onto his plate.

"That's all well and good," said the principal, "but education is what counts in the long run. And it's my job to see that these Indians stay in school. Now if Otis Chapman will listen to reason, he could make my job a lot easier."

Mr. Olson left the lunch room and went to a phone.

When the phone rang in Otis's studio, Jemmy was glad of the interruption, for her neck was stiff from posing. Otis had promised her a break every twenty minutes, but after the first two breaks he had become so absorbed in the portrait that he lost track of time, and she had been sitting now for nearly an hour in the same position.

"Yes, what is it?" he said brusquely into the phone. As he listened Jemmy saw his eyebrows rise, as though the caller had amazing news. "I hope he does," said Otis. "I hope he calls me; I'll be ready for him. And thank you for letting me know." He hung up.

"That was a former teacher of yours, Jemmy. A Mr. Olson."

She smiled, pleased that the two men she most admired knew each other.

"It seems the news about you and the Maiden has reached Eagleton High. He says he's happy you're the model."

She nodded. She could believe that. Mr. Olson always seemed to wish her well.

"He also says the principal might call and ask me to choose somebody else."

She caught her breath and turned away. She should have known this was too good to last.

"I hope he calls," said Otis. "It will be my first opportunity to educate a principal." He dipped his brushes into a bowl to paint thinner and dried them with a rag. "Let's break for lunch."

The kitchen phone rang as they lunched with Ann.

"Ah, yes," said Otis, "very kind of you to call . . . But I already have a Maiden; her name is Jemmy Stott . . . Yes, I am aware of that; she withdrew last Tuesday . . . Roxanne who? . . . She's going to earn a diploma? . . . Well, I'm afraid a diploma would disqualify Roxanne from being the Maiden. I hate to be the one to tell you this, but historians are agreed that the Maiden of Eagle Rock didn't have a high school diploma. Isn't that shocking? I was absolutely astounded when I heard. And of course my painting must be as authentic as possible. A girl earning her diploma would make the very worst model."

Then Otis laughed into the phone—a deep joyous roar—and when he hung up and turned back to the table Jemmy saw, for the first time, a broad smile in his beard and glee in his eyes.

Stott was asleep on the couch when Jemmy got home in the afternoon. He woke up dizzy.

"Where the hell have you been?" he said, getting slowly to his feet. "I've been out of smokes all day." He put out his hand for the denim jacket.

Jemmy took off the jacket and handed it to him. "I've been to the Chapmans' and I'll be going back there for another few days, so you'd better bring home extra cigarettes to see you through. And extra booze."

"You get chummy with that high-falutin' artist and I suppose the next thing we know he'll come waltzing right into this house." Jemmy had told her family about the Chapmans, and they aroused Stott's curiosity, though he tried to hide it under the guise of gruffness.

"I've thought of asking the Chapmans over, but our house is such a dump." Jemmy picked up the half-empty vodka bottle beside the couch.

"Well, if them Chapmans ever decide to pay us a call, just be sure and give me fair warning so I can make my getaway." He followed Jemmy into the kitchen.

"Are you going to be home for supper?" she asked. She set his bottle on a cupboard shelf.

He paused at the door and blinked several times, straining to see as far as suppertime.

"I like to know how many to cook for," said Jemmy.

He shrugged. Years of drinking had made him powerless to predict where he would be for meals. He put on the jacket and turned down the cuffs to cover his wrists. The jacket fit him almost as well as it fit Jemmy, for although he was taller than Jemmy his shoulders were very narrow.

"Well, I'll have something ready if you make it home," she said. She lifted the lid of the range and stirred the fire.

"Remember what I told you," he said, his hand on the doorknob. "When the Chapmans show up, make sure I get plenty of warning."

"Who says they're going to show up? I haven't asked them."

"Well, you might." He left the house.

Well, you might. Her father's tone struck Jemmy as strange. It was like a question. Could it be that her father wanted her to ask the Chapmans over, that he was suggesting it? Not likely, thought Jemmy. He had never brought home any visitors himself, and he never encouraged his children to do so. When Jemmy was little, Roxanne used to come over and play, but in the last several years the only callers at this house had been the property assessors from the county seat, and the woman from Eagleton who took the school census.

The next night, at supper, Stott brought up the subject once more. Jemmy was describing to Marty and Candy how still you had to sit when you posed for a painting, and her father said, "You haven't asked them over, have you?"

"No, because now that I've seen their house I'm ashamed of my own." There was a tinge of malice in Jemmy's voice, as though she wished her father to be hurt.

But Stott appeared unhurt. This was one of those rare days when his drinking had made him mellow. He pushed back his chair and looked about at the kitchen walls, at the soot stains over the range and at the paint chipping from the cupboards. He said, "No need to be ashamed. It's a fact of life that some people are rich and some people are poor."

"I don't think the Chapmans are rich," said Jemmy. "They just seem to live better on what they have."

"It's a fact of life that some people live in fancy houses and other people live in shacks." He smiled across the table, his eyes half-closed. It was the only smile his children ever saw him use—a stewed smile. "It's a fact of life that some people are lucky and some people are unlucky." He sensed that he was being profound, and he searched his fuzzy mind for another truth. "It's a fact of life that some people are sober and other people are drunk."

"And it's a fact of life that some drunks get sober and stay that way," said Jemmy. "They join Alcoholics Anonymous and they go along for years without a drop."

Stott kept smiling. "It's a fact of life that some women are naggers."

"What's a nagger?" said Candy.

"Jemmy's a nagger," he said.

"Our teacher's a nagger," said Marty.

"Was our mom a nagger?" asked Candy.

"Your mother was just a damn good woman," said Stott.

He left the table and went to the front room and switched on the TV. Marty followed him.

"Is Mrs. Chapman a nagger?" asked Candy.

"Call her Ann," said Jemmy.

She sat watching Candy eat her dessert, a dish of pears. She said, "Would you like to meet the Chapmans?"

Candy raised her head and nodded, pear juice running down her chin.

Painting the Maiden was the work of six days. Promptly at two o'clock each afternoon, Otis cleaned his brushes and Ann came into the studio and they sat with Jemmy before the canvas, drinking coffee and pondering the day's work.

On the first day the Maiden's face was entirely green, and it peered eerily out from a dark green background.

On the second day flesh tones began to appear, as well as the reds and golds of the blanket draped about Jemmy's shoulders.

Otis spent the third day working exclusively on the Maiden's eyes, and by two o'clock, because the rest of the face was still indistinct, the eyes pierced the viewer with startling intensity.

It was on the fourth day that the entire face came alive—the left cheek in sunlight, the right cheek in shadow, the glint of teeth through the slightly open lips, the hair partly in disarray as though swirled by the wind. The Maiden's expression was hard to define, contradictory, enchanting. There was anxiety in the brow, yet equanimity in the eyes. There was perplexity in the slight tilt of the head, yet determination in the set of the jaw. It was the expression of a girl working through grief and coming to a solution. It made Jemmy tremble to think that the Maiden's solution was suicide.

Otis devoted the fifth and sixth days, Friday and Saturday, to the body, and for this Jemmy stood in the same position until she was exhausted. Finally he allowed her to sit while he returned to the face, touching up small details. He added highlights to the sunlit cheek and the bridge of the nose and the hair. By working patches of cool blue into the green, he made the background recede, and this caused the planes of the face and the body, as though by magic, to take on a three-dimensional quality and stand out from the canvas like sculpture.

"Otis, I believe it's your best painting ever," said Ann.

Otis agreed, looking intently at his work, "Yes, the expression is exactly as I imagined it. I only hope I don't lose it in the mural, with the face six times as large."

Ann said, "What do you think of it, Jemmy? Aren't you pleased?"

"It's so real it gives me the shivers to look at it," said Jemmy. Never in a photo, not even in a mirror, had Jemmy seen herself so clearly. She had never thought of her face as particularly interesting, but she was fascinated by this replica, as though Otis's skill with shadow and color had given form to her soul, had put her feelings on display. For wasn't this the face of Jemmy Stott, after all? Call it the Maiden, call it a legend, but really the anxiety and perplexity were Jemmy's. And so was the steadiness.

"Do I look like that all the time?" she asked. "Is that my natural expression?"

"Yes, that's the way you look when you aren't thinking of how you look," said Otis. "Notice the steady eyes. The bold eyes."

"The pretty eyes," said Ann.

"But they're worried eyes. Do I look worried like that?"

"I wouldn't say worried," said Otis. "I'd say serious."

"And my hair. You've got a reddish color mixed in with the black."

"I paint what I see."

Otis went to his desk and wrote in a checkbook. He said, "The going rate for modeling is thirty dollars a sitting." He handed Jemmy a check. "And of course this canvas is yours when I am finished with the mural."

Jemmy read the check. A hundred and eighty dollars.

"We've got company," said Ann. Through the studio windows they saw a small silver sports car turn into the driveway and come to a stop under the oak.

"That's Miss Frost's car," said Jemmy. "She's the teacher at Reservation School."

Miss Frost and Roxanne Rooster stepped from the car. They knocked on the kitchen door, and Ann invited them in.

"I'm Frieda Frost and I've been so eager to meet the artist and his wife. Roxanne suggested we simply drive over and pay you a call." Miss Frost was a Zuni from New Mexico. She was twenty-six and new at Reservation School this year, having been chosen by the board for her youth and her enthusiasm for Indian culture. She wore her black hair in a thick braid down her back, and her earrings were silver spangles that flashed when she spoke.

She shook hands with Ann and Otis and said, "I'm thrilled to meet you." She took hold of Roxanne and steered her to the center of the room. "This is Roxanne Rooster, who lives across the road from my school. We're all very proud of Roxanne."

Roxanne, as though on wheels, came stiffly to a stop in front of Otis.

"How do you do," said Otis, a bit warily, recalling the principal's phone call.

Roxanne smiled and demurely lowered her eyes.

"Won't you have some coffee?" said Ann.

"We can stay only a minute," said Miss Frost, seating herself at the table. Roxanne and Otis joined her.

Jemmy, uneasy, stood in front of the fireplace, a hand at her throat as though to protect her necklace. In her other hand she held the check from Otis.

"We're really here for two reasons," said Miss Frost. "First, of course, we wanted to meet the artist and his wife, and second"—here she turned to Otis—"we would like to talk to you about Indian awareness."

Otis scratched his beard.

"A new day is dawning for the Indian. After a hundred years on reservations, we're trying to move into the mainstream of American life, and at the same time we're trying to hang on to the values and priorities of our ancestors. We like to do as much as we can for each other without being downright militant or anything like that."

This was the sort of attitude her mother would have admired, thought Jemmy. Both Miss Frost and Roxanne were proud of their heritage.

Miss Frost said to Otis, "Do you see what I'm getting at?"

"Not exactly," he said.

"What I mean is that we're all thrilled that your mural in Minneapolis will portray the Maiden of Eagle Rock. It will raise the level of Indian consciousness in all kinds of people for years to come. But let me ask you—you're the artist, after all, and it must be your decision—wouldn't the mural be more authentic if the model you used for the Maiden were a reservation Indian?"

Miss Frost looked from Otis to Ann to Jemmy to see if they all understood.

Ann was halfway to the table with the coffeepot and a plate of cookies when she caught the message. She stopped abruptly and looked at Otis, who was wearily rubbing his eyes.

"I'm sure you can see our point as Indians," said Miss Frost. "It's no reflection on Jemmy. I'm sure she'd be the first to admit that she doesn't feel a wholehearted commitment to the Indian people, and that's only natural because she has spent all her life *off* the reservation."

Jemmy held her breath. If Roxanne became the Maiden, she would die. Why was Otis saying nothing? Why was he not as prompt with his reply as he had been when the

83

principal phoned? Was he impressed by Miss Frost's argument?

Otis sighed and stood up and said, "Please come with me." He went into his studio with Miss Frost and Roxanne and he shut the door.

Jemmy and Ann sat down at the table. "And that's your best friend?" said Ann.

Jemmy shrugged, ashamed to admit it. "What do you suppose he's telling them in there? He isn't going to change models, is he?"

"Don't be silly."

In the studio Otis wasn't saying a word. He led Miss Frost and Roxanne around in front of the easel, and he let the painting speak. The effect on Miss Frost was instantaneous. The portrait, though scarcely larger than life, was a momentous presence in the room. Miss Frost knew artistic achievement when she saw it and she nodded her approval. At first, Roxanne looked askance at the painting, unwilling to be moved by its merits; but gradually the intensity of the Maiden's expression won her over and she too nodded.

"Does it not speak for your people?" said Otis.

Miss Frost said, "Yes, it speaks for all Indians. And for all maidens."

Roxanne said, "Nice," and she meant it sincerely, though she still felt cheated.

"We've got to be going," said Miss Frost.

Saying goodbye in the kitchen, Miss Frost shook Jemmy's hand and said, "Congratulations."

"Thanks," said Jemmy.

Roxanne was already out the door.

Driving away, Miss Frost said, "Now that I've seen the painting, I feel a lot better about it. And wasn't it a thrill to meet Otis Chapman?"

Roxanne was sick and tired of the whole matter. She twisted the rearview mirror so she could see her chin, which she examined closely. She said, "I never had a pimple that took so long to come to a head."

Through the kitchen window, Jemmy watched the silver sports car disappear down the road. Jemmy's entire experience with the Chapmans had been a joy, and now as she savored this new victory over Roxanne—Roxanne's Last Stand—she was moved to do something extraordinary. She turned from the window and said, "Can you come to my house tomorrow? It's Sunday and you can meet Marty and Candy. And my dad, if he's home." All week she had feared that her friendship with the Chapmans might not last beyond the painting of the picture.

Ann said, "Yes, we'd be glad to," and Otis said, "Of course."

And so, leaving the farm, Jemmy drove into town and bought cookies and pop and spent too much for a party tablecloth made out of paper.

At supper she told her family that company was coming and she wanted help cleaning house. Candy went excitedly to work with a dust cloth, and Marty, under duress, mopped linoleum. Stott opened a fresh bottle and drank himself to sleep.

The next afternoon Stott shaved and put on a shirt with no missing buttons. He took his place in front of the TV and although the Vikings were playing the Packers and reception was relatively clear, he spent most of the time looking out the window. He was curious to see the Chapmans. Did a famous artist and his wife look different from regular people? Did they talk different? What kind of car did they drive? Stott intended to escape to Rooster's Store for the afternoon and evening, but not before he got a good look at these strangers.

The Chapmans bounced along the driveway in their orange car and came to a stop beside the Dodge. Jemmy led her family outside and introduced everybody as they stood in the sunny, muddy yard.

Stott was overcome by a fit of self-consciousness. He shook Otis's hand and then Ann's, but he didn't lift his eyes from his shoes. "Pleased to meet you," he said twice, then got into the Dodge and drove away.

The Chapmans brought gifts. They gave Marty a three-bladed jackknife and a book about birds. They gave Candy a bracelet and a book about wildflowers. From the back seat of the car Otis drew out an easel and a paint box, and he said to Jemmy, "Show us where you want your studio."

Inside, he surveyed the kitchen and said, "Here, I believe this is your best light, near the window." He set up the easel in the corner near the sink while Jemmy opened the box and read the labels on the tubes of paint.

"You shouldn't have," she said. "We don't even know if I can paint."

"We'll find out mighty fast," said Otis. "I've decided I'm going to give you and Ann painting lessons at least twice a week between now and New Year's. You could both use the lessons, and I need something to divert my mind before I begin the mural."

Entering the Stott house, Ann was struck by the slanting floors and the wood-burning range and the old-fashioned corrugated washboard standing beside the sink. "Don't you have electricity?" she asked.

Jemmy said, "Sure," and she switched on the light bulb hanging over the kitchen table.

"That's not bright enough if you're going to paint in the evening," said Otis. "We'll have to get you something brighter."

Ann bent over the range. "You know, we were thinking of putting an antique like this in our kitchen, but I doubted if I could learn to cook on it. Does it have an oven?"

Jemmy showed her the oven.

"Isn't it hard to keep an even temperature for baking?"

"I don't know, I never bake. I mostly fry things. Or boil them."

Then there was a period of silence, and Jemmy felt awkward. Once you got visitors into your house what did you do with them? Ann must have anticipated this moment, for she drew from her purse a deck of cards and said, "Clear the table, everyone, and pull up your chairs. I'm dealing."

Old Maid was the ice-breaker. Halfway through the first hand Candy got the Old Maid and, with it, a frightful case of the jitters. She quit playing and crawled up onto Otis's lap. In the next two hands Jemmy was the Old Maid, which pleased Marty no end, then the Chapmans lost four hands between them, then Jemmy lost two more. Time after time, Marty avoided losing at the last moment and his excitement mounted steadily until the ninth hand, when he was finally caught with the Old Maid. He quit playing and went sulking into the front room, but when Jemmy spread the paper tablecloth and served pop and cookies, he was lured back to the kitchen by talk of a horse named Socko.

Chapter 8

November was cold, and December was colder. Beginning around Thanksgiving, a fine gray snow came sifting out of the low gray sky. The snow was driven by a cold wind and it swept through the forest and packed itself into the grassy fields until the earth was bereft of color and the winter birds were deprived of food. Each week Jemmy used seventy-five cents of the family's grocery money to buy birdseed. Flocks of blue jays and sparrows came to the feeder outside the kitchen window. They came in such numbers and in such hunger that the seed Jemmy carefully measured out each morning was gone by noon. A certain pair of blue jays seldom left the yard. When the feeder was empty, they perched on the bare twigs of a nearby tree, one above the other, and puffed out their feathers against the cold. The lower bird did a lot of squawking and looking in at the kitchen window, as though to shame Jemmy into providing more to eat. The higher one kept opening and closing its beak without making a peep, as if to say that Jemmy's neglect made it speechless. Every afternoon they sat there, hungry and watchful. Jemmy named the squawker Miss Frost. The other one she called Roxanne.

Jemmy visited the Chapmans three times a week—twice for painting lessons and once, on Saturdays, to let Marty and Candy ride Socko. Ann called on Jemmy nearly as often, for the dismal weather gave her need of diversion. Her visits were always announced ahead of time so that Stott could escape.

Jemmy and Ann began to learn more about one another's past. Jemmy's memories were mostly of happier times when she was going to Reservation School and her mother was alive. Ann talked about Otis and revealed a number of surprises. She said that she and Otis had not yet been married a full year. She said that Otis had been married twice before, that he had no children, and that he had been a college art teacher until his drinking got in the way of his teaching.

"Yes, to put it bluntly," said Ann, "Otis has a drinking problem. That was part of our reason for moving here, for buying a house—to leave his drinking companions behind. And it has worked out marvelously well. He hasn't had a drink since early summer. I'm as proud of him for staying sober as I am for his painting."

"Did drinking make him gloomy, like my dad?" asked Jemmy. They were in Jemmy's kitchen. Ann had brought her needlepoint and Jemmy was painting at her easel.

"No, he wasn't gloomy. At least not while he was drinking. Often after the drink wore off he was unhappy with himself, but when he was drinking he was always very friendly and talkative—and reckless. Otis is not naturally very demonstrative, you know, but when he drank he was a different person. He was wild, if you can imagine such a thing. No, his problem wasn't gloom, it was the opposite. He was sort of manic. He got extremely high-spirited and seemed to lose his sense of right and wrong. He threw his money away. He raced cars on the highway at night."

"Otis? I can't believe that."

"Thank goodness you can't. If it ever becomes believable again, that's when we're in trouble."

Birds fluttered past the kitchen window. Wind rattled the

door. The smell of woodsmoke was strong in the house, for Stott had been sold a truckload of green firewood.

"How did you meet?" said Jemmy.

"I was taking a summer course on the campus where he taught. We met at a concert."

"What did you do before you were married?"

"I taught third grade."

"For how long?"

"For ten years. Which makes me thirty-two, if that's what you're getting at."

Jemmy smiled. It was.

On another day, shortly before Christmas, Jemmy asked how old Otis was. This was in Ann's kitchen, where they were baking cracked-wheat bread.

"Otis is fifty. Would you believe it?"

"Yes, I would have guessed fifty."

"Really? His beard is so black, I think it makes him look younger. His beard is new. He grew it when he quit drinking. He said if he was going to *be* a different man he was going to look like a different man."

"It's hard to imagine how he'd look without it."

"I'll show you a picture." Ann went into another room. There was the sound of laughter from the yard, Otis's laughter as well as Marty's and Candy's. They were riding Socko up and down the driveway.

Ann returned with a photo album. She laid it on the kitchen counter and opened it to a page where Otis stood, beardless, in the gothic archway of a college building.

"He looked younger without the beard," said Jemmy.

Ann did not reply. She went to the kitchen window and looked out. She was silent for a long time, then said, very softly, "I don't like to admit it, Jemmy, but your Minnesota winter is beginning to get me down. The days are so short, and the snow never melts. Looking out this window, I think of those pioneers in *Giants in the Earth*, and I understand the strength it must have taken to endure those bleak winters on the prairie. I wonder if it was wise of them to leave civilization so far behind and live that lonely life on the frontier. I sometimes wonder the same about myself."

Jemmy was sitting by the fire, looking at the album. "You've got Otis," she said.

"But Jemmy . . . Otis has been acting strange lately. Quiet and withdrawn. I don't know, it scares me a little. I never saw him like this before."

"Maybe it's the mural."

"Yes, of course. As the time draws near, the mural occupies his mind more and more, and I suppose it's only natural, but some days it's spooky the way he'll go along for hours without saying anything. What's he thinking, do you suppose?"

"Hard to say."

"Some days I worry about him."

"When he starts painting he'll probably snap out of it. He's always friendly when we're here."

"Naturally, with visitors around it's different." Ann turned from the window, and her voice brightened. "And speaking of visitors, we're having a few people in over New Year's. Some friends from Chicago are coming up for the holiday, and on New Year's Eve we're inviting a few people out from Eagleton as well. All of you Stotts are invited."

Jemmy shook her head. "I don't know. It sounds like we'd be out of place."

"Nonsense, you must come."

"But we never go to parties."

"Do come. Everyone will want to meet the Maiden."

Every New Year's Eve, six or eight families from the reservation gathered at Rooster's Store for a party. It was an uproarious affair that began in the house and spilled over into the store and lasted until 2:00 A.M., when the nation's final midnight celebration—the West Coast celebration— was broadcast on TV. Ordinarily Stott attended this party

91

without his children, but this year, to their amazement, he asked them along. He was sitting with them at supper when he said, "How about the four of us going to the Roosters' party tonight? There'll be a lot of other kids."

Marty was eager to go, for Rollie Rooster had received a toy racetrack for Christmas.

Jemmy said, "If I went to a party it would be to the Chapmans', but I guess I'll stay home and paint. They're having a bunch of strangers over."

"Suit yourself," said Stott, nibbling on a crisp noodle, which he had drawn out from under his chow mein. He was seldom hungry.

"What about you, Candy?" he said. "Put on your coat and come along."

Candy looked from her father to Jemmy and considered the alternatives. It was sure to be a dull evening at home because Jemmy spent all her time painting these days; yet in spite of Roxanne's fascinating cosmetics collection Candy was reluctant to go. She associated Rooster's Store with her father's sour disposition.

"I'll stay with Jemmy," she said, choosing dullness over sourness.

Stott gave her a snort of disappointment and ate another noodle. He wished Candy would come along. He wanted to show her off to the mothers from the reservation who thought him a failure. He wanted them to see how pretty she looked wearing the new jacket and sweater the Chapmans had given her for Christmas.

Curious people, the Chapmans. As he waited for Marty to finish eating, Stott sat back and folded his arms and stared at the light over the table—no longer a bare bulb, but a light inside a frosted glass ball. It was a present from the Chapmans. Too bright, in Stott's opinion, but Jemmy insisted it was necessary for painting pictures. Stott resented Jemmy's spending so much time at the Chapmans' house, especially since she had begun taking Marty and Candy along. Stott had been invited too, of course, but he never considered accepting. How could he, a drunk, pass an afternoon or an evening in a house so fancy that his kids couldn't quit talking about it? And besides, Otis Chapman—if you could believe what people said—was a reformed alcoholic. What would a reformed alcoholic think of the likes of Stott? He'd probably preach at him.

Only once did his kids pressure him to go to the Chapmans', and that was for brunch on Christmas morning. But Stott had stood his ground. He had stayed home and watched TV, glad of the peace and quiet; Marty and Candy had been on vacation for a week, and every day they seemed to take up more room and make more noise than the day before. When they came home from the Chapmans' that day, they were loaded down with presents. Besides new sweaters and mittens and books and toys, they brought home four new jackets, including one for Stott himself. These were expensive jackets, unlike anything sold in Eagleton. They were filled with goose down and they had detachable hoods. At first Stott refused to accept his jacket, but at Candy's insistence he tried it on, and it made him feel so warm and comfortable that he couldn't imagine going back to the denim jacket with the tattered cuffs. He talked himself into keeping it, convincing himself that the artist owed him this jacket in return for the use of his daughter as a model.

But Stott resented the rest of the gifts, particularly the books and toys. Kids could be easily spoiled by all that stuff. He wished the Chapmans would mind their own business. Who did they think they were, anyhow, luring his kids away from the life they were used to? It had all started in October when they rescued Jemmy from the blizzard. After that, the Chapmans came barging into the Stotts' lives like uppity relatives. Sometimes Mrs. Chapman came right into this house and helped Jemmy with some frilly nonsense like hanging curtains in the kitchen. Whenever she paid a call, Stott went out to the Dodge and hightailed it down the road to Rooster's Store, where Stan Rooster consoled him.

"Kick her out," Stan would say. "A man's house is his castle, and he has a right to keep meddling strangers off the premises. Go home and kick her out."

"My kids wouldn't stand for it," Stott would say. He knew a lost cause when he saw one. Jemmy would keep seeing the Chapmans no matter what he said, and so would Marty and Candy. Jemmy was crazy about the Chapmans, and Marty and Candy were crazy about their old horse.

"Who's boss in your house?" Stan Rooster would say. "Your trouble is that you aren't boss in your own home. If my seventeen-year-old daughter started telling *me* what to do, I wouldn't stand for it."

"Let's have another drink," Stott would say, knowing that Stan was right. Stott didn't have much control over his children anymore. Control had somehow passed from him to Jemmy after she quit school. This was something he hadn't foreseen. He had assumed that by quitting school she would simply have more time for cooking and cleaning house and tending to the little ones. He hadn't expected her to start calling the shots.

Well, he could live with it—as long as she didn't nag him. He drew the line at nagging. He had tried to make that clear to her on the day of the Chapmans' first visit. He had come home that Sunday evening after the Chapmans had left and hung his jacket on the new easel in the kitchen. Jemmy got huffy. She told him to keep his things off her easel and then she went on to scold him for never helping to keep the place neat, for scattering his clothes all over the house. "Shut up!" he shouted and he stomped out the door and he went straight back to Rooster's. A few days later, she told him he needed a shave. "Shut up!" he shouted again as he disappeared out the door. Then one day she said he had no table manners. She said Otis Chapman had manners. That was the last straw. He stood up from the table and took his plate of food and smashed it on the floor. That was a message she seemed to understand. There were mashed potatoes spattered on the wall. After that, she didn't nag him anymore.

"Why don't you eat your chow mein?" Candy asked her father. Under the bright globe of frosted glass, Candy's hair looked orange.

"How can anybody eat with the house smelling of turpentine?" he said. "Are you ready, Marty?"

Marty nodded and left the table. He and his father put on their new jackets and went out to the Dodge.

Stott knew by the way the car acted that it was very cold. The engine growled before it started, and it coughed all the way to Rooster's Store. He parked among half a dozen other cars on the packed snow of the schoolyard and followed Marty across the road. Stan Rooster's outdoor thermometer, nailed to the front door, said twenty-eight below zero.

After Marty and his father left for the party, Jemmy washed dishes and then brought in several armloads of wood for the kitchen range. There was already a fire in the oil burner in the front room, but on nights this cold an all-night fire was needed in the kitchen to keep the pipes under the sink from freezing. In the front room Candy sat on the couch and wrapped herself in a blanket to watch TV. Jemmy sat down before her easel in the kitchen and studied her latest painting—a view of Eagle Rock from across the Turtle Egg River.

This painting was based on the sketch she had done nearly two months ago—the day Otis had given her the sketchbook, the day they had seen the eagle. Now the scene, without the eagle, stood here on the easel, and she found it both pleasing and troublesome. She was pleased with the way the sky was reflected in the water and with the way the cliff stood up from the far shore, but she was having trouble with the three birch trees in the foreground. With

Otis's help, she had finally learned how to make a proper pencil drawing of a tree (if your paper had enough tooth, each grain of pencil lead became a leaf) but producing a tree with oil paint was another matter. These three birches looked to Jemmy like three soup ladles standing on their handles.

This was Jemmy's eighth painting. In the two months since Otis began giving them lessons, Ann's interest had flagged and Jemmy's had grown. Hardly a day passed that Jemmy didn't paint, either at the Chapmans' or at home. Some days she lost herself in her work the way she used to become lost picking berries—but with a difference: when you were lost in a painting you weren't so eager to find your way out; everything was fascinating—the colors, the shapes, the textures. Often, as she painted here in the kitchen, she became so absorbed that hours passed like minutes. Sometimes, thinking it was midday, she had been astonished to look up and find Marty and Candy coming in from school and the light fading in the western sky.

Four of her paintings were hanging, unframed, in the four rooms of the house. There was a creek scene in the kitchen and a hill of trees in the front room and there were barns in both bedrooms. She kept three of her paintings in her closet because they were so rotten. One was a view of Reservation School in which the proportions seemed fine but the colors turned out too vivid and the road refused to lie flat. Another was a forest scene, and here the colors were muddy. The third failure was a still life—a vase and several apples—that she hadn't been able to finish because her family kept eating the apples.

Now as she toiled away at the birch trees, Candy came into the kitchen, dragging her blanket behind her. "There's a horse on TV," she said. "He looks like Socko."

"Is that so?"

"He has three white feet and one dark one, just like Socko."

Jemmy nodded absently, her eyes on the painting.

"Can we go ride Socko tomorrow, Jemmy?"

"Too cold. We'll wait till it warms up."

"Can we get a horse someday, Jemmy? Marty says we could keep it in the shed."

Jemmy shrugged, lost in her painting.

"How come we aren't going to Otis and Ann's party?"

"They're having a lot of people we don't know."

"But if we went we'd know them."

They heard a car in the yard and Candy went to the window.

"It's Otis and Ann's car," she said, doing a little dance, wrapped in the blanket.

Otis Chapman came in with frost on his beard. "I'm here to collect all the Stotts I can find." He swung Candy into the air, her heels grazing the ceiling. "Come on, Jemmy. There are people at our house asking for you."

"Asking for me? Who's asking for me?"

"All kinds of people. They've seen your portrait and they will give me no rest until I deliver you to them. Put on your coats and bank the fires and come along, all of you. Where's Marty?"

"He went to Rooster's with Dad. They're having a party."

"It's a night for parties. We'll see the New Year in, and I'll deliver you both home in the wee hours. What's this?" He was looking at the easel. "Why, it's Eagle Rock as seen from across the river. And very good. But these birch trees, Jemmy. You're piling up too much paint. There's a trick to painting birches."

With a palette knife he scraped away layers of wet paint, then using white paint on the edge of the knife he made three swipes at the canvas and produced three birch trunks standing up from the water's edge.

"Tricks," he said. "Painting is tricks."

Next he dipped a brush in a mixture of purple and brown

and he touched the canvas with the ends of the bristles, producing the illusion of bare twigs.

"Leafless trees demand a light touch, Jemmy. There. Now it's ready for you to sign your name. But not now. Your public is calling for you."

Jemmy combed her hair and put on her jacket.

At the Chapman house every window was alight, and the door, when they opened it, let out a blast of off-key singing.

In the kitchen Ann handed Candy a Coke and Jemmy a glass of champagne. Otis poured himself a cup of coffee.

In the parlor Jemmy was introduced to a plump, gray-haired woman. "How nice to meet you," said the woman. "It was my husband who recognized your portrait. 'That's Jemmy Stott,' he said. And then Otis explained to everyone that you were the model and that you lived nearby, and, of course, hearing that, everyone insisted that you join the party. Here comes my husband now."

Her husband was Mr. Olson. He advanced upon Jemmy, giving her the same smile she had hoped for every day in history class. "What good fortune that you and the Chapmans found each other in the blizzard," he said. "Otis tells us that yours was the very face he had been searching for." Unlike the other guests, who were dressed casually, Mr. Olson wore one of his classroom suits, and, as in the classroom, he rose on tiptoe as he spoke. "And not only that, Jemmy, but Otis tells us that you paint. You can't imagine how glad I am to hear it."

Ann came along in a minute and led Jemmy and Candy into the studio. The room was full of people and Jemmy forgot most of their names a moment after meeting them. On champagne she grew suddenly bold, and when she overheard a man saying that hers was the perfect face for the mural, she interrupted him to ask why.

"Well, I would say it's your natural expression." This was a bald man wearing a copper medallion around his neck, a painter Otis had known in Chicago. "An artist looks for the face with the interesting expression," he said. "Not a posed expression, mind you, but an interesting *natural* expression. I would say your natural expression is very . . . interesting."

A woman in green spoke up. "In my opinion it's the depth in your eyes. Who wants to look at a portrait of someone with shallow eyes? Depth is what it's all about, honey, and you've got it."

"It's the Indianness of her face," said a young man in a red sweater. "You may be right about the depth, but this girl's face is the classic Indian face. The cheekbones. The eyes."

Jemmy held out her glass for more champagne.

"It's her guilelessness," said Mr. Olson, who had followed her into the studio. "You can see at a glance that there's not a speck of guile in her."

Next time I'm in the Eagleton Drug Store, thought Jemmy, I'll have to look up "guile" in a paperback dictionary.

"Let's ask the artist," said someone. And they did.

"All right, I'll tell you why I chose her," said Otis. He led Jemmy to the model's chair and asked her to sit. He stepped back and, with his guests, he regarded her for a moment in silence. During that moment, Candy left Ann's side and went to stand next to her sister. Jemmy put her arm around Candy's waist.

"Now there's a picture for you," said the bald man. "If I were sober at the moment I'd make a sketch."

"You ask about her face," said Otis. "I heard you all speculating, and I think you're all correct. You say I chose her because she is Indian. You're right, of course. That had to be a primary consideration. You say it's her interesting expression, and that too is correct. I needed an interesting expression, and I hope Jemmy doesn't mind my saying that something a little on the sad side was what I was looking for—an expression slightly troubled; for the Maiden of Eagle Rock has just lost her true love, remember—and there is that hint of melancholy in Jemmy's eyes. In the way her mouth turns slightly down. Wouldn't you agree?"

Everyone agreed.

"And what you say about the lack of guile is certainly true. I had to have a sincere face, an innocent face. To the person looking at the mural, the face must say 'maiden,' and Jemmy's does."

"It does indeed," said the young man in the red sweater.

"And finally the depth," said Otis. "Don't you see seriousness in those eyes? Deep feeling? Gravity? Those are the eyes of someone who knows there's more to life than TV and potato chips."

"A peerless face," said the bald man. He sounded drunk. Most of the guests, in fact, were high on champagne, and before Otis had quite finished speaking they began chattering and turning their attention to other matters. Candy soon grew sleepy and was put to bed. As midnight approached the chatter began to sound to Jemmy like the high-pitched gabble of excited geese, and when the clock struck twelve she was kissed four times—once by the bald man from Chicago, once by the young man in the red sweater, and twice by Otis.

Just as a serious painter develops a style of painting, so a serious drinker develops a style of drinking. Stott's style was to grip his bottle of orange-flavored vodka in one hand and a glass in the other and pour his troubles into the ear of whoever would listen. All evening at the Roosters' party, he had been pointing out, in slurred and bitter words, how his unhappiness could be blamed on his children, on the Chapmans, on the county welfare director, on the governor of Minnesota, and most of all on the late General Douglas MacArthur, under whom he was serving in Korea when he suffered a crippling case of battle fatigue. His talk grew loud and foul and most of the Roosters' guests—those in the house as well as those in the store—tried to avoid him.

"Boy, your dad is really wasted tonight," Rollie said to Marty as they sent the tiny race cars speeding around the track. They were playing on the drafty floor under the front window of the store.

Marty pretended he didn't hear Rollie's remark. He was aware of the strained feelings his father was causing among the guests, and he wished he had stayed home. Now he heard his father and another man raise their voices in anger.

"Boy, listen to that," said Rollie. "What's it like to have your old man drunk all the time?"

Marty lunged across the racetrack and hit Rollie in the eye. Rollie fell back, stunned, and Marty ran to the door. By the time Rollie got to his feet and looked out the window, he saw Marty crossing the road in the icy moonlight. Marty was not wearing his jacket. No one else had noticed Marty's departure, and Rollie decided to say nothing about it. Instinct told him that it was dangerous to be outside for long on a night this cold, yet if he told his parents they would want to know what caused the fight and he wasn't about to repeat what he had said.

Across the road Marty disappeared among the cars parked in the schoolyard. He wanted to be alone. He didn't like being at a party where his father was acting like a fool. His pockets were jammed with candy and cigarettes. He would enter the schoolhouse by way of the belfry and start a fire in the stove and have himself a peaceful New Year's Eve, eating and smoking.

Outside the schoolhouse, Marty trembled with cold. He wished he had brought his jacket, but to have gone into the Roosters' living room for it would have delayed his escape from Rollie. The cold steel of the flagpole burned his hands as he climbed it. He lost tiny patches of skin where his fingers were moist and they froze to the pole. From the flagpole he scrambled to the peak of the roof and removed the false bottom of the belfry. He dropped into the black attic. Shivering, he felt around for the trapdoor and pulled it open. By the moonlight slanting through the windows of the classroom he could make out the center row of desks. He let himself down through the trapdoor and hung by his fingers for a second. Because they were numb, he lost his grip and dropped before he was ready, but by kicking in the air he was able to land safely in an aisle.

He stood up and looked about. The classroom was spooky. It was frozen in a cold, blue light. His fingers hurt. He stood for a moment with his hands between his thighs, trying to warm them. Then he lifted a book off the teacher's desk, tore out a handful of pages, and threw them into the stove.

But he had no matches—he had forgotten matches.

The teacher kept matches. He tried the drawers of her desk but they were locked.

He went to the back of the room where the eighth-grade boys sat—the ones who smoked—and he searched their desks but found no matches.

He had never been so cold. He put his hands inside his shirt, under his arms, but instead of warming his hands this made him cold all over. His shivering turned to quaking. He cursed himself for not remembering matches. He would have to leave and come back some other night. Some night when it wasn't so cold. Now he would return to the store and face Rollie, who was probably waiting to punch him back. And he would have to put up with his father's stupid behavior. At least in the store it was warm.

He opened a window to climb out. It was barred. A heavy steel screen was fixed outside this window and all the others. He had known that. He had forgotten.

He broke into a sweat of fear which quickly froze and made his shirt stiff. He pushed on the strong wire mesh. It wouldn't budge. He went to the woodbox, brought out a stick of oak, and rammed it against the steel screen again and again, but it made scarcely a dent.

He shouted, "Hey! Hey! Hey!" He shouted ten times, twenty times, a hundred times. His voice got smaller as he shouted. In the moonlit schoolyard the cars, wearing a thick coat of frost, stood facing him like polar bears.

"Hey! Hey! Hey!" he shouted. Across the road, warm yellow light poured from the windows of Rooster's Store. Shadows crossed the windows and now and then Marty could hear a whoop or a laugh, muffled and distant.

"Hey! Hey! Hey!" His voice was hoarse. He stood at the window and watched the moon follow its slow path down the sky. He fumbled in his pocket and drew out a candy bar, but his fingers were wooden and he couldn't tear the paper. He dropped it to the floor. Suddenly there was a great roar across the road, and the shadows in the windows became more animated. Midnight, he thought.

"Hey! Hey! Hey!" His voice was a whisper.

It was two A.M. before Marty was missed. Then there was a twenty-minute delay in finding him because Rollie wouldn't let out the secret that the school could be entered through the roof. However, when Rollie's father took off his wide leather belt and threatened him with a whipping, he had no choice. Marty was found lying on the floor unconscious, his hand gripping—and frozen to—a leg of the cold stove.

At three A.M. when Otis drove Jemmy home (Candy asleep in her arms), they found a car standing in the Stott yard with its motor running. It was Roxanne Rooster and Morrie Benjamin, necking. Roxanne rolled down her window.

"What are you doing here?" said Jemmy.

"I'm supposed to tell you that Marty's in the hospital in Eagleton. He froze one of his hands real bad. The doctor says he's pretty sure he'll have to cut off two of his fingers."

Chapter 9

Marty lost the fourth and fifth fingers of his left hand below the second knuckle.

And he lost his spirit. After ten days in the hospital he came home a different boy. He brooded over his three-fingered hand. It was a humiliating hand. Not only was it different from everyone else's, it was a reminder of how stupidly he had got himself trapped in the schoolhouse. He refused to let anyone see the hand except Jemmy, who changed the dressings every day. He refused to return to school. He refused to leave the couch in the front room.

Ann Chapman stayed home from Minneapolis in order to be of help. Each day she visited the Stott house, and each day she sat down next to the couch and tried, in vain, to break through the shell of Marty's despair. His eyes remained fastened on the TV screen, even when the picture was blurred, and nothing Ann spoke of, not even Socko, brought a glimmer of response to his face.

In late January the Reservation School Board sent messengers to the house to lure Marty back to school. They sent two eighth-grade boys, they sent Rollie Rooster, and finally they sent Miss Frost.

With cigarettes dangling from their lips, the eighth-grade boys shivered on the back step as they explained to Jemmy what they had come for.

"Marty's not ready to go back to school," she told them, and she sent them away.

The next day Rollie knocked on the door and said, "I'm supposed to talk to Marty."

Jemmy let him in. He went into the front room and stood before the couch in his parka and mittens and overshoes and said, "Miss Frost says either come back now or don't come back at all."

Marty took his eyes from the TV and lay face down on the couch.

"Ain't you coming back at all?"

Marty covered up his head.

"Well, I came all this way. At least show me your hand."

"Marty's not ready to go back to school," said Jemmy, and she ushered Rollie out the door.

Two days later, during one of Ann's visits, Miss Frost arrived in her silver sports car. She came into the kitchen and shook Ann's hand and said to Jemmy, "I'd like to speak to Marty. I'm afraid his absence is getting us all in trouble."

Jemmy showed her into the front room, and Marty, as though sickened at the sight of her, hid his face.

"Marty, you've got to come back to school and I'll tell you why. It's only by permission of the governor that Reservation School is allowed to remain open. All the other one-room schools in Minnesota have been closed by law and the students transported to larger schools, but Reservation School is being kept open as an experiment. The Chippewas asked the governor to let them keep it open so they could teach Indian values, Indian culture, and the governor said okay as long as a high level of attendance was maintained. But now, Marty, you're spoiling the school's good attendance record. You're jeopardizing the existence of Reservation School."

Marty burrowed deeper into the couch. Miss Frost saw that it was no use talking to him, and she went back to Ann and Jemmy in the kitchen.

"I know this sounds harsh, but the school board says if he doesn't return in a few days he'll have to be expelled. Technically, you see, if he's expelled then he's no longer absent."

"He's not absent if he's expelled?" Ann studied Miss Frost for signs of a joke. "Are you serious?"

"It's a technicality."

"If he's expelled, how is he supposed to learn to read?" said Jemmy. "He doesn't read very well yet."

"If he's expelled he'll go to school in Eagleton. Actually that would be better all around. You may not realize it but the board has been making a special exception in allowing Marty and Candy to attend Reservation School. Not only are Marty and Candy half-white, they live *off* the reservation. We have a few half-whites in school who live *on* the reservation, but your brother and sister are the only half-whites living off. According to regulations both of them should be going to Eagleton."

"Is that a technicality too?" said Ann.

"Yes, it's a board regulation. But in the case of Marty and Candy they made an exception, because the Stott family seemed so down and out, Mr. Stott being a . . . you know, having that disability. But if Marty can't be a credit to our school, then the board can't be expected to carry him. Our school is a testing ground for Indian education. The Bureau of Indian Affairs has its eye on us."

"He can't go to Eagleton," said Jemmy. "He'd have to get used to a whole new bunch of kids. And all those strangers on the school bus."

Ann said, "He'll have all he can do to go back to *your* school. Eagleton would be impossible."

"Eagleton was about impossible for *me* when *I* went there," added Jemmy. "And I had ten fingers."

"I understand that," said Miss Frost, "but I want you to see our side of it too. Please do what you can to see that he comes back to school in the next few days."

"He won't be ready in a few days," said Jemmy. "Yesterday I got him to leave the couch for the first time and come into the kitchen for his meals. That was the first step. Next I'm going to try to get him outdoors, maybe to the Chapmans', maybe to Eagleton. But not to school. At least not yet."

Ann said, "He wants no one to see his hand except Jemmy. Not even his father or Candy. What he needs right now, Miss Frost, is understanding—not school."

"School *is* understanding," said Miss Frost.

"Only in theory," said Ann.

Miss Frost quit arguing. "All right, I'll tell the board that Marty will be absent awhile longer. But I can't promise you anything."

She said goodbye and went out the door and across the yard, her thick pigtail bouncing on her back. She got into her silver sports car and drove away.

Jemmy stirred the fire in the range. It was that time in the afternoon when Ann usually went home and Jemmy started supper.

"Don't you ever cry?" Ann asked, her eyes wet.

"No," said Jemmy.

"Don't you ever *feel* like crying?"

"Yes."

Ann put on her coat, but she didn't leave. She sat down on Jemmy's painting chair (today the picture on the easel was a view of the Chapmans' farm) and she said, "Jemmy, I've got to tell you something. I'm going to join Otis in Minneapolis. I'm driving down this weekend."

Jemmy nodded.

"After Marty froze his fingers I told Otis I would stay here at the farm as long as you needed me, even till spring if necessary, but I can't stay any longer, Jemmy. I just can't endure the winter—the snow, the lonely life. Some mornings I wake up and think if I don't get to the city immediately I'll go to pieces. I don't see how you do it, Jemmy. I don't see how you *stand* this life."

"It's what I'm used to. I belong here and you belong with Otis."

"I feel like I'm deserting you, Jemmy, but Otis has been gone a month and I simply can't live alone on that farm another week. I've got to go."

"You aren't deserting me. You'll be back, won't you?"

"Yes, we'll drive back on weekends. We've talked it over and decided to drive up to the farm every Saturday morning and go back to the city every Sunday night. And then in about two months the mural will be finished and we'll take you to the city for the dedication." She wiped her eyes. "Otis says he's making marvelous progress."

"Has he started the Maiden?"

"No, the Maiden will be last. He's finishing the background—the cliff and the river—and he says it's turning out even better than he expected. I'm dying to see it."

"Me too."

"And of course you *will* see it, when it's finished."

Jemmy dropped a stick of wood into the range.

"Now, Jemmy, we've got to talk about Marty." Ann lowered her voice. "Is he ever drawn out of himself? Does he ever laugh?"

"At TV sometimes."

"He's got to be drawn out of himself, Jemmy."

"I know. It will come."

"It won't come by itself. He needs a push. He needs Socko."

"What do you mean?"

"When I'm gone Socko and the chickens will need to be fed. I had thought of hiring someone to come out from Eagleton to feed them and keep an eye on the place, but I see now that tending to the horse and the chickens would be the perfect job for Marty. Could you take him to the farm each day we're gone and put him to work, Jemmy? Have

108

him feed the horse and clean the stall? Have him take chicken feed out to the hen house? You could show him how it's done. It would take him about twenty minutes a day, and we would pay him."

"I'll do it for you. I'm sure Marty wouldn't want to. Not yet."

"He's got to." Ann stood up and looked into the front room. She went to the door and stood there, about to leave. "I'll be driving down to the city this weekend. I feel terrible leaving you alone."

"We'll be okay." Jemmy was cranking open a large can of beans.

"Promise you'll take Marty to the farm each day. The thought of that will make me feel better when I'm gone."

"If he'll go, I'll take him. That's the most I can promise." She dumped the beans into a pot.

"Oh, Jemmy, you're so . . ." Ann searched for the word, but couldn't find it. "I'll see you tomorrow." She turned up her fur collar and left.

At the sound of Ann's car leaving the yard, Marty came into the kitchen. He wore his blanket over his head like a hood. "When's she going to Minneapolis?" he asked.

"Sunday, I guess."

"Then I start feeding Socko on Monday, right?"

On Monday afternoon Jemmy drove Marty to the farm but she did not put him to work. Instead she put a bridle on Socko and helped Marty up onto his back and turned the two of them loose in the barnyard. The horse sauntered around, stopping here and there to paw through the crusty snow for a taste of frozen grass.

"Ride him down the driveway and see if there's anything in the mailbox," said Jemmy.

She watched them move slowly away. At the mailbox, Marty leaned down, hanging on to Socko's mane, and drew out a handful of letters. He then drove his heels into Socko's ribs and they returned to the yard at a trot. Marty handed the letters to Jemmy. With his mittens on, he seemed to have forgotten about his hand. Jemmy saw something like happiness in his eyes.

"Can I ride him down the road a ways?" he asked.

"Yes, down to the first crossroad and back." She watched them go. She noticed how naturally Marty rode. He leaned slightly forward on the horse, one hand holding the reins and the other patting Socko encouragingly on the side of the neck. From a distance it appeared that Marty was speaking, and Socko, perking his ears, seemed to listen.

The next day Marty helped Jemmy clean Socko's stall and feed the chickens, then he rode again to the crossroads. Jemmy, using the key Ann had left with her, went into the house to warm herself. The empty kitchen looked forsaken. The table and chairs stood stiffly before the empty fireplace. She went into the studio and this room, too, seemed hollow and dead. Gone were all the sketches and paintings Otis had done in preparation for the mural. His easel had been put away. She went to the window to let in daylight, and as she put out her hand to draw back the curtains—before she quite touched the curtains—she had an extraordinary feeling. It was more than a feeling; it was a vision. She saw in her mind the fields and the trees and the road that lay on the other side of these curtains, but she didn't see them as they were now, covered with snow; she saw them as they would be in May or early June—the oak and birch leafing out and all the birds back from the South and dandelions blooming in the ditches. Yet she imagined that while the world outside was flowering, the studio and kitchen were dark and empty. No furniture in the house, no one at home. So vivid were the details of this premonition—the green of early summer outside, the echoing stillness inside—that Jemmy held her breath as she drew the curtains and she sighed with relief as she looked out at the frozen land.

Impulsively she picked up the studio phone and dialed the number Ann had written on a note pad.

"Hampton Hotel," said a voice.

"The Chapmans' room," she said. "The Otis Chapmans."

The phone clicked and buzzed, then Ann said hello.

"Ann, this is Jemmy. I'm calling to ask a question."

"Are you calling from the farm? Is Marty with you?"

"Yes, he's riding Socko."

"Oh, I can't tell you how good that makes me feel. And you're calling to ask where the scoop shovel is for cleaning the stall. I forgot to tell you it's hanging behind the door in the barn."

"No, we found the shovel. I'm calling to ask if you and Otis are planning to move away from here."

A pause. "I wish you had called about the shovel, Jemmy. That would have been much easier to answer."

"Well, I just came into Otis's studio and had a very strong feeling that you weren't going to live here again. It was like seeing the future. It was summer and your house was empty. Emptier than it is now. The rooms were all bare. Is that going to come true?"

Another pause. "I can't say right now, Jemmy. Otis likes the wilderness. He did some of his best work of his life up there, and if he insists I'm sure we'll go back. But, Jemmy, I walk down these city streets and I'm reminded all over again that the city is my element. And Otis can see that. We went to a concert last night, and afterwards Otis said, 'The country is nice, but I guess the city is where we belong.'"

"So what I just saw is probably going to come true."

"Now don't worry about it, Jemmy. We haven't made any plans. If we can afford it, maybe we'll have two places and divide our time between the country and the city. I wish you wouldn't worry about it."

"I'm not worrying. What will happen, will happen. It's

just that my vision was so real I wanted to see if there was anything to it."

"It's too early to say. Now tell me about Marty and Candy and your father. And Socko."

"Marty is different when he's on Socko. He's better."

"I knew it. It's too bad you don't have a barn at your place. You could take Socko home. And your father? How's your father?"

"He's at Rooster's Store most of the time, as usual. Yesterday he did something strange. He brought home a bunch of comic books for Marty. Somebody at Rooster's Store told him comic books helped kids learn to read, and he drove all the way to Eagleton for them."

"He's a good man at heart, Jemmy. He should be encouraged to take up his house painting again. I've been thinking that when spring comes we should hire him to paint our barn . . . And Candy?"

"She's fine. She reads better than Marty. Last night he asked her to read one of his comics to him."

"Candy is steady. She's going to be like you, Jemmy."

"Could be."

"Jemmy, you should see the mural. It's breathtaking. Otis has finished the background, and he's about to paint the Sioux brave, and when he finishes that he'll start on the Maiden. Your face alone will be six feet high, can you imagine? The colors he's using are gorgeous. They're fall colors, because the battle was fought in the fall, you know, and you can see Eagle Rock standing up across the river and at the base of the cliff there's this autumn haze. When you look at the mural you can almost smell the way it is on a warm autumn day. Promise you'll come with us to the city and see it when it's finished."

"I'll come."

"You should see all the people in the Courtyard, Jemmy. It's a very busy place because the Tower is full of shops and offices. All day long people stop to watch Otis work, and sometimes when he comes down off the scaffold they applaud. It's very exciting."

Ann's excitement was obvious in her voice. She went on to describe the clothes he had bought, a movie she had seen, and people she had met. Her talk gathered momentum; her words came crowding and rushing over the phone like city traffic, and Jemmy interpreted them to mean that Ann would never again leave the city for long. How could Ann Chapman, city born and bred, be expected to return to this house and look out this window, as Jemmy was doing now, and see this snow-covered yard, these snow-covered fields, this icy road, nothing alive and moving as far as the eye could see except—way off in the distance—a boy on horseback?

Later when Marty and Jemmy returned home, they found in their mailbox a letter addressed to their father. At supper Stott opened it, read it, and handed it to Jemmy. It was an ultimatum from the Reservation School Board. Marty would return to school by the following Monday or transfer to the fifth grade in Eagleton.

Without looking up from his soup, Marty felt himself being stared at by his father and Jemmy. He slowly removed his three-fingered hand from the table and hid it in his lap.

Jemmy went to the stove, lifted the lid, and dropped the letter into the fire. She said, "Tomorrow, Marty, you and I are going to clean out the shed. And, Candy, you will help us when you get home from school. We're going to make room in there for Socko."

"Socko? In our shed?" Marty's head jerked up.

"Socko? In our shed?" echoed Candy.

"And the day after tomorrow, if it's nice, Marty will ride him over here. It's about three miles. I'll haul a sack of oats and as many bales of hay as we can get in the trunk of the car."

"Socko in our shed?" said Candy, giggling.

"Socko in our shed?" said Marty. He put his thumbs in his ears and wiggled his fingers, forgetting he had only eight.

After supper Stott went to Rooster's Store but he didn't stay long. He was home by eight, pulling Stan Rooster's two-wheeled trailer behind the Dodge.

"For cleaning out the shed," he explained to Jemmy as he passed through the kitchen. "And for hauling hay." He sat down with Marty and Candy to watch TV.

Jemmy left her easel and joined them in the front room. She watched her father as well as TV. He sat on the couch and appeared oddly content to have Marty leaning against his right shoulder, Candy against his left. His hair, fading from red, was unruly and there was an unhealthy pallor in his face, but his eyebrows, for a change, were not drawn into a troubled scowl. Was it possible that he had been as distraught over Marty as Jemmy had been? And was his relief as great as hers now that Marty's spirit was beginning to heal? When had the four of them last watched TV together, she wondered. Or done anything else together, for that matter. She felt a sudden surge of fondness for her father and brother and sister, and she went to the kitchen and popped a large pan of corn and did not object when Marty and Candy ate it very slowly, delaying their bedtime.

The next morning Jemmy backed the two-wheeled trailer up to the shed, and by the time Stott rose from his bed at noon she and Marty had taken two loads of junk to the dumping ground and were prying up old nails and pieces of broken glass from the floor of frozen earth. Stott came outside and went to work fashioning, from his old painting ladder, a gate to be hung across the doorless doorway of the shed.

As they worked side by side, Jemmy told her father that

when the weather warmed up the Chapmans would like to have their barn painted.

"That so?" he said.

"By you," said Jemmy.

Stott raised his eyebrows, surprised that anyone should think of him as a painter—it had been so long.

"Will you do it?" she asked.

He shrugged.

"Will you at least look the barn over and talk to Otis about it?"

"Hard to say. Spring's a long way off."

"Promise me you'll at least talk it over with Otis."

"I guess I could do that. No harm in talking it over."

Stott, Marty, and Jemmy worked on the shed throughout the afternoon, and when Candy came home from school there was nothing left to do but speculate.

"Is the door high enough?" said Candy. "Will Socko have to bow his head to get in?"

"It's high enough," said Marty.

"Is it wide enough? His belly is kind of big, you know."

"It's wide enough."

"It isn't very warm in there."

"Jemmy says horses don't need heat. They just need to be out of the wind."

"I don't think there's enough room for him to turn around in there. He'll have to stand facing the back wall all the time."

"He won't care," said Marty.

"Maybe we could back him in."

"No, Jemmy says horses want to have their rumps to the weather."

"Rumps to the weather." Candy giggled.

The next afternoon was sunny and almost too warm to see your breath. At the Chapmans' farm Jemmy and Marty loaded the trailer with hay and oats and buckets. They put the eight chickens into two gunny sacks and tied them shut and set them on the back seat of the car.

Then, just as Marty was about to mount the horse, Jemmy put her hand on his shoulder and said, "The reason we're taking Socko home is so you can ride him to school every day."

"School?" Marty's face clouded.

"You've got to promise you'll go every day, otherwise we leave Socko here."

He struggled against his sister's grip.

"Promise," said Jemmy.

He turned his head away and mumbled something.

"Are you promising?"

Marty said either *Yeah* or *No*, Jemmy couldn't tell. "That's good," she said, pretending it was *Yeah*. "I'll tell Miss Frost to expect you in the morning. You can tie Socko to a tree in the schoolyard."

"Help me up," said Marty.

She boosted him onto the horse and they set off for home. At first Jemmy followed behind in the car, but this made the horse uneasy, and Marty waved her around them. She passed them and drove slowly in the lead. Socko didn't mind having the car ahead, but Marty did. In the mirror, Jemmy saw him waving frantically, indicating that she should get along home and not worry about him; let him ride alone. She guessed he was right; she was being overprotective. She speeded up and left him behind.

Marty and Candy arrived home from opposite directions at the same time. They met at the mailbox. Marty pulled Candy up behind him on the horse and gave her a ride along the driveway into the yard. They dropped down off Socko's back, took off his bridle, and lured him into the shed with handfuls of hay. They hung the ladder-gate in place behind him.

"Look how good he fits," said Candy.

"Tomorrow we're riding him to school," said Marty.

* * *

And they did. Socko carried Marty and Candy to school and received—at noon hour and during both recesses—a full measure of fond attention. It didn't take Marty's schoolmates long to figure out that only those who ignored his missing fingers were permitted on Socko's back for a ride around the schoolyard.

Chapter 10

It was an early spring. By late March the migrating birds had returned from the South. There were crows in the fields and ducks in the swamps. Loons called from the lakes and owls hooted in the forest. Although Jemmy had quit setting out birdseed as soon as the snow was gone, a great many blue jays, cowbirds, and grackles made daily flights past the feeder, hoping to find a meal.

On the last Saturday in March the Chapmans arrived home for the weekend and found their lawn carpeted with robins. They carried their suitcases into the house, and as Ann was perking a pot of coffee she heard a timid knock at the kitchen door.

It was Stott.

"You?" she said, unable to hide her astonishment.

Stott nodded, averting his eyes. He wore a white cap advertising Dutch Boy Paints, and with a trembling hand he clung to its bill as though he were standing in a wind.

"Come in," said Ann. "We'll have coffee."

"No, I'm here about the barn."

"Oh, you've come to paint it!" She threw her arms wide and Stott, fearing she would embrace him, stepped back.

"No, I ain't here to paint it. I'm here to say how much it will cost if I *do* paint it."

"Oh, I'm so glad."

"Is Chapman in?"

"Otis, it's Mr. Stott."

Otis, shaking Stott's hand, pulled him indoors. "Sit down and have a cup of coffee, Mr. Stott. Do you take cream? Sugar?"

"Neither one."

At the table, Stott didn't remove his cap but continued to cling to it. He was in misery. Ever since Jemmy first proposed painting the Chapmans' barn, he had had nightmares about being trapped in this house with the famous artist and the artist's wife. He had promised Jemmy that as soon as spring came he would look over the barn and estimate the cost of the job—and then, to his sorrow, spring came early.

"Are Marty and Candy still riding Socko to school?" asked Ann.

He nodded.

"We can't tell you how glad we are that things worked out for Marty. Your children can keep Socko as long as they wish. He's theirs."

Stott nodded again, his eyes on the tablecloth.

"Have you lived here all your life, Mr. Stott?" Ann served coffee and tried to draw him into conversation. "I can see where a native might be fond of the wilderness, because when the weather is nice, like today, there's a certain charm about it. But Otis and I, we've found that we're fond of this area only part time."

"I ain't very fond of it myself," said Stott. "Colder'n hell in the winter." He lifted his cup shakily to his lips and splashed coffee on the tablecloth.

"Have you looked at the barn?" said Otis.

"Yep, looked at it this morning." Stott put down his cup.

"How many gallons of paint will it take?"

"Twelve. Three gallons to a side, four sides, that's twelve gallons."

"And shall I buy your equipment? Brushes? A ladder? Turpentine?"

"I got brushes. I know where I can borrow a ladder. I used to have a ladder of my own, but I cut it in pieces to make a door to keep the horse in the shed." Stott quit trembling and began to relax. As long as the subject was painting, he was on firm ground. "I figure it will cost you three hundred and sixty dollars. That sounds high, I know, but I don't come close to charging what they charge in town. If you had somebody from town come out and paint that barn, you'd pay them a damn sight more than three sixty. I ask less because I ain't what you'd call the fastest worker."

"I understand," said Otis.

"I can't be on a ladder for long at a time. My lungs and legs ain't good. You should know about that from the start. When you get me to paint something you ain't getting speed. What you're getting is know-how."

"I'll take know-how over speed every time." Otis examined Stott's face—the interesting lines, the unhealthy color—and he imagined the portrait he might do of it. He was reminded of studies he had made of his own face before he had hidden these very same lines behind his beard.

"And you've got to consider the scraping," said Stott. "I don't know if you've noticed, but there's a lot of chipping paint to be scraped off that barn. There's some jobs where the scraping takes longer than the painting, and this looks like one of them. So what I'm thinking is somewhere around twenty hours per side, scraping and painting. Four sides is eighty hours, and my charge per hour is four fifty. Eighty times four fifty is three hundred and sixty dollars. Plus the paint."

"You're behind the times," said Otis. "I'll pay you a total of five hundred. Here's your first installment." He drew five twenties from his billfold. "And if you'll buy the paint I'll pay you for it."

"You want red?"

"Yes, red."

Stott took the money and stuffed it into his shirt pocket. He raised his cup with barely a tremor.

Ann asked, "Are the chickens laying a lot of eggs, Mr. Stott?"

"We get one egg a day."

"Goodness, we used to get more than that."

"Well, you had more chickens. We already ate four or five hens."

On Monday morning Stott drove into Eagleton, bought twelve gallons of red paint, and had enough money left over for six bottles of vodka.

On Tuesday he borrowed Stan Rooster's ladder and deposited it, along with the paint, in the Chapmans' barn. Tuesday afternoon and all day Wednesday he drank.

On Thursday he worked for two hours, scraping the chipped paint from two window frames.

On Friday afternoon, shortly after arriving at the barn, he grew drowsy in the sun and lay down on the ground and snored until the sun sank behind the trees and he was awakened by the chill shadow that fell across him.

On Saturday when the Chapmans arrived from the city at noon, Stott was high on the ladder, scraping the weathered siding under the eaves. He looked down at the orange car as it came to a stop under the oak. The Chapmans got out and Ann said something sharp across the roof of the car to Otis. Stott didn't catch the words but they sounded angry.

Otis walked over to the barn. "How's it going up there?" he called.

"She's going to soak up a lot of paint," said Stott, glad of this excuse to come down to solid ground and rest. He had been on the ladder an hour and his feet ached. "My estimate might have been a little on the shy side; she's going to soak up paint like a blotter."

"That's all right. It will fall to ruin if it isn't painted."

"Look here," said Stott. "I'm going to have to reputty." He led Otis on an inspection of window frames. They circled the barn. Stott pointed to old swallow nests, knotholes, and rot. They stopped near the barn door and examined the rusty hinges. Stott offered Otis a cigarette.

"No thanks, never touch them anymore."

Ann approached them from the house. She was scowling. She said, "Hello, Mr. Stott."

Stott gave her a nod and lowered his eyes and gripped his Dutch Boy cap. He had a Chapman on each side of him and he sensed a current of uneasiness running between them.

"Are your children at home?" she asked.

"Yep."

"Good. I'll drive over and pick them up and we'll have a picnic in the yard. Up here on this farm I feel a great need to gather people around me." She hurried to the car and drove away.

"Anyhow, Chapman, I was hoping to be farther along by now, but the weather put me behind. There was a couple days of bad wind, and then my war trouble acted up. I was in Korea in fifty-one and I ain't been the same since. I get tired. I don't breathe so good."

"And you drink too much!"

Stott jerked back his head as though he had been slapped.

"Admit it, Stott. You've been drinking too much for years. When you're drinking, you're no good to anybody, least of all yourself."

Stott worked his wrinkles into a sneer. Smoke streamed from his nostrils.

"When you're sober you're a man with a profession, Stott, but when you're drunk you're a bum."

Stott threw down his cigarette and stomped around the corner of the barn.

"All I want you to do is admit the truth," said Otis, following at his heels. "The day you can say to yourself,

'I'm a drunken bum,' that's the day you can quit being a bum. You've been using the Korean War as an excuse for drinking for twenty-five years. You haven't put in a day's work all this week. I should have hired Marty to paint this barn. He'd have done a hell of a lot more than you have."

Stott turned another corner.

"I can say this to you, Stott, because for twenty years I was the same kind of bum you are. I drank for twenty years, and you know what it cost me? It cost me two wives and four teaching jobs. You hear me? Two wives and four jobs. My first wife was named Doris and she stuck it out for thirteen years before I drove her crazy. My second wife was named Helen and she stayed with me for nine weeks. She was smarter than Doris. She gave up quick before I ruined her life."

Stott came to the ladder and climbed it.

"How many lives have you ruined, Stott?" Otis was looking up at the soles of Stott's shoes. "Just one, as far as I can see—your own. You're lucky. It looks to me like your three kids are going to turn out all right. Jemmy can take care of herself and she can take care of Marty and Candy. I don't think you can ruin any of them, Stott. I think they're going to make good in spite of their father. It's only yourself you're ruining. Which means that when you decide to quit drinking you've got only one life you have to repair."

Stott reached the top of the ladder and wished he hadn't climbed it. He felt like a treed cat.

"Stott, do you realize there is a state in this country where I can never again apply for a driver's license as long as I live? I was arrested so many times for drunken driving in Illinois that they finally made it illegal for me to own a car. I'll bet you never heard of that before, Stott, forbidding car dealers, statewide, to sell a man a car. Can you imagine what a bum I must have been?"

Stott, enraged, grew suddenly dizzy and had to cling tightly to the ladder and close his eyes. He would have fallen to the ground had Otis not climbed up and helped him down.

"I got to go home," said Stott, allowing Otis to guide him to the Dodge. He climbed in behind the wheel.

"I'm sorry," said Otis, "but damn it, Stott, I can't stand to see a man throw his life away."

Stott shook his head, woozily. He started the car.

"I don't think you should drive. I can take you home when Ann gets back. Why don't you come into the house until you feel better."

Stott put the car in gear, turned in the yard, and drove away. Halfway home he met the Chapmans' car, full of his family. They waved at him. He reached home and parked between the shed and the house. He walked over to Socko, who was staked out in a patch of brown weeds.

"I'm going to quit drinking," he said.

The horse lifted its head and looked at Stott sideways. A skeptical look.

"I mean it," he said. "I'll show that famous bastard."

While Marty and Candy went up into the Chapmans' hayloft and threw down several bales to take home to Socko, Jemmy went into the house and helped Ann prepare the picnic.

Otis, sitting at the kitchen table, told them what he had said to Stott.

Jemmy's reaction was a shrug.

Ann's was alarm. "You mean to say you called him a drunken bum to his *face*? A man who lives from day to day on the smallest ego I've ever seen in my life? Are you trying to destroy him?"

Jemmy was shocked by this combustion of feeling. As her father had earlier, she sensed the high voltage moving between the Chapmans today.

Otis said, "It takes a jolt to turn an alcoholic around. You

124

know that, Ann. You remember when I lost Helen and I lost my job at Central State."

"But it's not the *same* in this case. Jemmy's father is a very weak man. You were never a weak man, Otis. You were weak only in the area of drinking. Otherwise you were always very strong, very creative. You had those other things going for you. What does Mr. Stott have going for him? Good Lord, you've probably destroyed him!" Ann was dicing onions for potato salad, chopping them with a heavy cleaver.

"Ann, I know he's a weak man, and I also know that you can't build from weakness. When you're as weak as Stott you have no foundation to build on. You can build on anger or you can build on regret—any genuine strong emotion— but you can't build on weakness. If he's angry, that's good. He can turn that anger into will power. If I got him to regret his wasted years, that's good too. He can turn *that* into will power."

"You're very calculating, Otis. You play with people's lives."

Jemmy left the kitchen. She went outside and lit a cigarette and sat on the doorstep. Waiting for the Chapmans' raised voices to subside, she felt her spirit sink. Through the open doorway she heard Ann say, "Don't you see he was already started on the road to recovery when he agreed to paint the barn? And your lecturing him has destroyed his faith in himself?"

Otis said, "But in five days he accomplished next to nothing. A man in his condition can't paint a barn."

Jemmy was grieved. Her father's temper and Roxanne's treachery never hurt her the way the Chapmans' eruption of bad feeling was hurting her now, and she wondered if she had made a mistake in becoming fond of them. But how could she have helped becoming fond of the Chapmans? They had been so good to her. They were so easy to like.

It was a dismal picnic. The Chapmans said very little to

each other, and Marty and Candy, after stuffing themselves with potato salad and hot dogs, begged to be taken home so that they could ride Socko.

"We'll go as soon as dishes are done," said Jemmy. She went into the house with Ann.

"Forgive our bickering, Jemmy, but it's been a tough week in the city." Ann was standing at the sink, running dishwater. "Dedication day is almost here, and Otis is working twelve and fourteen hours a day on his painting, and some days I wonder if he remembers that I exist. There's more to being an artist's wife than meets the eye, Jemmy. It's clear to me now that Otis is married to his art as well as to me. It's a little like bigamy."

"Is he going to finish in time?"

"Yes, as far as I can see, it's finished now; but he keeps going over it, changing little details. He's spent over a week on the Maiden's face—changing her complexion, changing the way her hair falls around her shoulders. You'd think he'd be sick of the whole business, he's been at it so long— twelve weeks in the city to say nothing of the time up here making sketches—but no, he's up on that scaffold every day, spending hours and hours on little things that the viewer will hardly notice."

"Are you in the Courtyard while he paints?"

"I'm in and out. I drop in and we go and have a snack, but even then Otis is often very remote. He'll have a faraway look in his eye, and although we might be five blocks away from the Courtyard I know what he's looking at. In his mind's eye, he's looking at the mural. I say, 'Snap out of it, Otis, it's only paint and plaster; please don't lose your mind over it.' And do you know what he says to that? He says it's his supreme work."

"It must be beautiful."

"But his supreme work, Jemmy! What does that say about his next work? And the one after that? When he says

126

that this is his supreme work, it sounds like he's planning to go downhill from now on."

"Maybe every work is his supreme work, while he's working on it." Never before, with Ann, had Jemmy felt such a need to choose her words with caution. "I know when I'm painting a picture I lose interest in it if I don't think it's going to be my best one yet."

"All right, I can see that. But this time Otis is obsessed. He'll come down off the scaffold sometimes and sit on a bench and stare at the mural for a half hour at a time. And people will be going by, looking at the mural and looking at Otis, and you can tell what they're thinking. You can tell they admire the painting—and it really is beautiful—but you can also tell that Otis frightens them. He's sitting there with such a forbidding look on his face that they give him a lot of room when they walk by."

"That doesn't sound like Otis."

"Well, as I say, we're seeing a side of Otis we didn't know was there. Like today, with your father. Did *that* sound like Otis? Calling somebody a drunken bum?"

"Don't worry about my dad. A jolt might be just what he needs. Nothing else ever worked."

"Jemmy, you keep contradicting me. Whose side are you on?"

"Whose *side*? Do I have to be on a side?"

Ann hung her head over the sink of suds and closed her eyes. "I'm sorry, Jemmy."

Jemmy put down her dishtowel and slipped out the open doorway, but Ann didn't notice.

"Do you see how scared I am that Otis might turn out to be different from the man I married?"

A robin chirped just outside the doorway.

"Jemmy, do you understand?"

A crow called from the pasture. Ann lifted her head and found herself alone. She went to the door and saw Otis and the three Stotts getting into the car.

They were nearly home before Jemmy spoke. "I've never seen Ann like this before."

Otis tried to smile but it looked more like a cramp in his cheek. "It's nothing serious, Jemmy. It's our first real tiff. We're still newlyweds."

"Did something bad happen this week in the city?"

"No, something wonderful—I finished your face." Now his smile was genuine. "It's my supreme work, Jemmy. I have never painted on such a large scale before, nor have I ever been so happy with the outcome. Nor have I ever worked so hard. I had difficulty with your skin tones and your expression. I was standing too close to see what I was doing, and again and again I had to climb down off the scaffold to see how it was coming. Wait till you see it. Your face dominates the entire Courtyard. It stops people in their tracks."

Otis turned into the Stott yard and came to a stop behind the Dodge. Marty and Candy jumped out and ran to the horse. Jemmy remained in the car.

"So the Maiden's face turned out as good as the portrait?"

"Every bit as good, Jemmy. I see people stop and look up and I sense an instant bond established, as though you were speaking to them. And you *are* speaking to them—with your eyes. Sooner or later all of Minneapolis will pass under that mural, Jemmy, and they will all pause as you speak to them."

She felt giddy at the thought of speaking to all of Minneapolis. "What do I tell them?"

"You tell them you've lost your lover. Your message is melancholy."

"That's not much of a message." She opened her door.

Otis lost his smile. He felt wounded by her remark. He reached for her hand, which she drew away from him, feeling vaguely resentful—she wasn't sure why. Was it

128

because of his spat with Ann? Was it because he had called her father a drunken bum? Could it be that she was offended when her father was offended? Or was it something harder to pinpoint? Despite the lovely weather, this whole day had been unlovely. People's voices seemed harsh and off-key. It was a day for getting things off your chest.

"I've never found it easy to believe in the Maiden of Eagle Rock," she said, "not even after *being* the Maiden of Eagle Rock. I've always thought there was something a little sappy about her."

"Sappy!" Otis was puzzled.

"I sometimes think my sophomore history teacher was right. I think we ought to be careful about believing every legend that comes along."

"What do you mean, sappy?"

"I mean her suicide. People have to be crazy to commit suicide. What's so great about a girl killing herself? Are we supposed to respect her for that?"

"It's a romance, Jemmy. It's a pretty story. Can't you let yourself be carried away by a romantic story? I swear you're acting just like Ann today. Her mood must be contagious."

"I just wish that as long as I'm speaking to all of Minneapolis I was saying something besides 'Give up.'"

"What would you rather be saying?"

She thought for a moment. "I'd rather be saying, '*Don't* give up.'"

Otis nodded. "That would be Jemmy Stott speaking, all right. 'Don't give up' is exactly what I would expect you to say—something as forthright and sensible as 'Don't give up.' But the Maiden must not say that, Jemmy. When you pose as the Maiden you must say what the Maiden says. And the Maiden says, 'Alas.'"

"I suppose you're right. But do you see what I mean?"

"Yes, of course. You will never really fit the image of the Maiden. Instead of leaping off Eagle Rock after the battle, you would have gone home and cooked a meal for your family. The Maiden lacked your strength. And your grace. In the mural I am portraying only one side of you, Jemmy— your gravity. I do not portray your grace. Your ability to carry heavy burdens as though they weren't heavy. Your manner of moving gracefully through obstacles as though you didn't recognize them as obstacles. Remember the eagle the day you sketched Eagle Rock? Your grace is like the grace of that eagle, Jemmy, the way you turn and climb and glide through life. Where did you learn that grace?"

Marty was trying to release Socko from the stake he was tied to, but the knot was too tight. He called to Jemmy for help.

"I've got to go," she said. She moved to get out of the car.

"Jemmy, is your father likely to be stewing in there? Do you want me to come in and talk to him? Apologize?"

She shrugged. Long ago she had given up trying to determine what was best for her father.

"I could apologize if it would make it easier on you and Marty and Candy."

"Don't worry. He'll be okay."

"All right, till tomorrow then. Ann and I will stop here tomorrow on our way back to the city. We want to talk to you about the dedication ceremony."

"When is it?"

"It's Wednesday, and we won't be able to come up for you. Monday morning Ann and I are flying to Arizona to talk over plans for another mural. They want to commission me to do an Indian scene for a college down there. We're flying down Monday and coming back to Minneapolis on Tuesday. The dedication is Wednesday. We're arranging for you to ride down with some people from Eagleton. They're coming down early Wednesday morning, and they'll pick you up and bring you along."

"Who are they?"

"Miss Frost and the mayor of Eagleton and his wife."

Minneapolis was four hours away. That was a long time to be in the same car with Miss Frost and a mayor. She said, "I don't know."

"What don't you know?"

"I don't know if I want to go down with them."

"But it's essential that you be there for the dedication. After all, you *are* the Maiden. Would you rather ride down alone? On the bus? I can buy you a bus ticket if you'd prefer."

Marty called again. "Jemmeeee."

"Think it over," said Otis. "We'll settle it tomorrow. Ann and I will stop by in the late afternoon."

She nodded and shut the door. She watched him back out of the yard.

Behind her, Stott was watching too, scowling through the kitchen window.

Marty and Candy called together: "Jemmeeeeee."

All day Sunday a fierce wind swept across the fields and rushed through the forest. The sky was a cold blue and the wind-torn clouds were a dingy yellow—a mixture of sunshine and dirt. In the afternoon Jemmy sat at her easel and worked on what she considered her best painting to date, a lone oak tree in a snowy field.

"Why are you painting a wintry tree?" her father had asked. "It's spring. There's buds on the trees."

"Why are you painting snow?" asked Marty. "The snow is gone."

"It's so *dull*," said Candy.

To make it less dull, Jemmy added specks of rust where dead leaves remained on the boughs, but that was her only concession to popular taste. She was concentrating on simpler compositions these days, fewer colors. This canvas was almost a monochrome: shades of gray with a hint of blue in the sky and snow. This was the oak that stood at the crest of the Chapmans' driveway, but on this canvas she had transferred it to a level field of snow, where its balance showed to better advantage. It was the balance of the oak that fascinated her. During the winter she had sketched the tree from several angles and had come to understand— through the close observation that sketching demands—its pleasing symmetry. From whichever side you looked at the tree, its masses of twigs and boughs were of equal weight and you were convinced that each twig, though twisted into a shape of its own, had come into existence to balance a twig on the opposite side of the trunk. Here, as Otis had once pointed out, was random growth forming a pattern. "The artist finds the pattern," he had said when he was giving her lessons. "Most people see a random world, but the artist sees the patterns."

Now, through painting, Jemmy was beginning to understand what her mother had meant about nature being one's guide. Sometimes when it was hard to keep your balance in life, it helped to look at a tree like this oak—to study its strength and balance. And to look at eagles. Didn't Otis say yesterday that Jemmy had the grace of an eagle—that her climbing through life reminded him of the eagle's flight? Obviously that's what her mother had meant about learning from nature—that trees and birds were models to imitate. How interesting that Otis, an artist from Chicago, should conceive of nature the way her mother had—as though Otis were an Indian. As though her mother were an artist.

The wind howled as it funneled itself between the house and the shed, and occasionally it carried a shout or a laugh from the yard, where Marty and Candy were brushing Socko. But for a long time Jemmy didn't hear Marty or Candy or the wind. She was deep in her painting, lost in its patterns. Each time she worked on this canvas she had only to pick up her brush and she was immediately crossing the snowy field and coming to rest in the mazy lacework of oak twigs—where this afternoon she remained until she heard a commotion beyond her father's bedroom door. Her father made a sudden, alarming noise, like a cry of pain.

Jemmy went to his door and called, "What's the matter?"

"Go away," he growled.

She returned to her easel, but the sound of his agony—if that's what it was—continued. It kept her from reentering the painting. What was he doing in there? she wondered. Was he trying, single-handedly, to cure himself of drinking? Was he having convulsions?

She heard him curse and cry out.

She looked at the clock on the wall. The Chapmans would soon arrive. She cleaned her brushes and put on the denim jacket and left the house. She walked along the road, leaning into the wind that rustled the roadside weeds and hummed through the power lines overhead. A half mile from the house she left the road and walked into the forest and climbed a small hill. It was one of the few hills in an otherwise level landscape, and from it she could look through the tall pines and see the house. Marty and Candy and Socko were tiny in the yard. The chickens were white specks. Two miles beyond the house she could make out Reservation School and Rooster's Store.

She saw the Chapmans' car arrive in the yard. She saw Otis and Ann follow Marty and Candy toward the house. She put her hands out in front of her nose and formed a frame with her fingers. She was pleased to see how small Otis and Ann and their car appeared in the vast landscape. That, for the time being, was how she preferred to think of them—small and far away. She had allowed herself to become too close to the Chapmans. If she had kept her distance, as was her instinct, yesterday's angry words— even if they were a harmless tiff—wouldn't have saddened her so. If she had kept her distance she wouldn't be expected to go to Minneapolis for the dedication, where she would no doubt be expected to stand up in front of a lot of people. She didn't want to put herself on display. She would

133

rather pass up the dedication. She wanted to see the mural, of course; she wanted to confront herself as the Maiden; but she could do that any time. She could go down in the Dodge someday with Marty and Candy.

The Chapmans' car remained in the yard for a half hour, and when Otis and Ann finally gave up and drove away it was at a crawl, both of them scanning the fields for Jemmy. By this time the wind was dying, and a bank of dark clouds had moved up from the horizon and swallowed the sun. When the car was out of sight, Jemmy left the forest and walked home.

"Ann wrote a note," Candy told her as she entered the house.

"When do we eat?" said Marty.

Jemmy broke several eggs into a frying pan and set it on the range. She picked up the letter. It was written in Ann's precise, teacherish hand. Clipped to the letter was a twenty-dollar bill.

Dear Jemmy,

Where are you? There's so much to tell you but it's getting late and we must be off to the city.

You can come to Minneapolis either by car or by bus. Miss Frost and the mayor and his wife are driving down on Wednesday morning, and they have assured us that you are welcome to ride along. Miss Frost will visit you on Tuesday to see what your plans are. Or you can take this $20 and buy a ticket on the early morning bus. If you wish to stay overnight we will reserve a room for you at our hotel. Whatever you decide, please phone us tonight at the hotel. The phone at the farm, as you know, is still connected, and you have the key.

Tomorrow we leave for Arizona. We'll be back on Tuesday. Then on Wednesday, immediately after the dedication, we fly to St. Louis, where another mural is in the works. Otis is suddenly in great demand, and it's obvious now that we won't be keeping the farm. We're putting it up for sale immediately. We'd like to take our time relocating, but the realtor in Eagleton says early spring is the best time to sell a farm. So don't be shocked when the *For Sale* sign goes up. It doesn't mean we're leaving you forever, Jemmy. We'll return to pack our belongings. And even after we move we'll be sure to keep in touch.

Sorry for yesterday's tempest in a teapot. Otis and I have talked out our troubles and all is well. I guess we're both in a state of nervous excitement as the dedication nears. And as new opportunities present themselves.

Sorry to have missed you this afternoon. Where have you gone?

Awaiting your phone call.

Love,
Ann

Jemmy folded the letter. That was a lot of news all right. She gazed out the kitchen window. Behind her, in the front room, she heard Marty and Candy turn on TV. She heard her father emerge from his bedroom, coughing. Outside she saw a hawk—or was it an eagle?—floating over the forest; then she lost sight of it as a sudden shower of rain made the window opaque—a small cold rain falling with the darkness.

Chapter 11

Monday morning Stott, looking terrible, was up early enough to join his children at breakfast. It seemed to Jemmy that his wrinkles had deepened over the weekend and his hair had whitened, yet his hands were unusually steady. She wondered if he had quit drinking. Was that why he had been groaning in his room yesterday? And, if so, was it possible for a person to dry himself out in one day?

"Pack me a lunch, Jemmy," he said. "I'm going to put in five or six hours on that barn today."

"Let me drive you there," she said. "I need the car for shopping." She made him two sandwiches, twice his normal lunch. She didn't tell him that the farm was to be sold. A day's work—or at least attempting a day's work—would be good for him.

The four Stotts left the house together, Marty and Candy on the horse, heading for school, Jemmy and her father in the car.

Jemmy came to a stop under the Chapmans' oak and saw that no *For Sale* sign had yet appeared on the property. She watched her father go to the barn and climb a ladder, a paint scraper and a wire brush sticking out of his back pockets. The climbing sun was already warm, and she rolled down her window. She heard a string of crows calling to each other as they dipped and rose over the pasture.

In the afternoon when she returned to the farm for her father, she found him sitting under the oak, smoking. She saw that one entire end of the barn was covered with fresh red paint.

"I don't know if I should of took on a job this big," he said, easing himself into the Dodge. "There's some dry rot under the eaves on the south side. It's going to be more work than I thought. At least if I'm going to do it right. I suppose I could paint over the dry rot. I've been known to do that. But this here's a good barn. She's square and she don't leak. God, I'm tired. I ain't put in a day like this since before your mother died."

They both sat looking through the windshield at the barn.

"It looks nice," said Jemmy.

"Not bad, if I say it myself." He tugged at his cap. "Another couple weeks she'll look like new. Tomorrow I'll start on the south side."

Jemmy was tempted to tell her father that she was proud of him, but she didn't trust the words. They were words other people might say, Otis or Mr. Olson or a character in a book, but not a Stott. "It's nice," she said again.

At supper Stott ate two pork chops and two helpings of fried potatoes and he lectured the children on the merits of hard work and fresh air. He was tired but talkative, as though standing all day on the ladder had given him a broader view of life, shown him courses of action that had seemed impossible when he was idle. He said that when he finished the Chapmans' barn he was going to paint his own house and shed. He said it was a good enough house and it ought to be taken care of. True, it leaned a little, but it was snug and the roof didn't leak. He told Marty that he would help him fence off the half acre behind the shed so that Socko could be turned loose to graze instead of being tied to a stake all the time. He said he knew where he could get a load of fenceposts cheap.

After supper he drove to Rooster's Store, refused an

137

invitation to drink, and came straight home with an odd, long-handled tool that he said was a post-hole digger. He took Marty outside in the twilight and showed him how to use it.

The next morning Stott set off to work in the Dodge, but he was back home in twenty minutes. He told Jemmy that a realtor was putting up a *For Sale* sign at the foot of the Chapmans' driveway.

"I'm not surprised," said Jemmy. She was hanging clothes on the line. A warm wind was lifting her hair and whipping the sheets.

"It ain't fair," said Stott, leaning against the Dodge, his arms folded, his cap pulled low over his eyes. "I was just getting a good start on that barn. The realtor said the Chapmans talked to him on Saturday and put the place up for sale. He said they're going to look for a new place down South somewhere. Way South. I think he said Arizona."

"So you're going to quit painting?"

"What choice have I got? I said to the realtor, 'What am I supposed to do about the barn? She's partly painted and partly not,' and the realtor said, 'They didn't say anything about the barn being painted,' and I said, 'Well, I'm damned if I'll paint a barn and not know if I'm going to get paid what's coming to me,' and he said, 'Suit yourself.' Then I said, 'Maybe whoever buys the place will want me to finish it,' and he said, 'Could be.' He said he'd contact me if the new owner wants me to finish the job. So I loaded up the car with what paint was left—seven gallons—and I'm going to put it on our own place—house and shed."

"You're going to paint the house red?" asked Jemmy.

"House and shed."

"I'd like white, at least for the house."

"The paint's bought."

"We can exchange it. I'll take it to town and exchange it. We'll start scraping today."

138

"Exchange it if you want." Stott untied the rope that held the ladder on the car.

Jemmy and her father spent the day removing chipped paint from the siding of the house. After school Jemmy gave her scraper to Candy and went inside to start supper. Candy and her father chatted as they worked, and Jemmy listened through the open window.

"Don't stand under me, Candy. You're getting flakes of paint in your hair."

"I am?"

"Did I ever tell you that my hair used to be the same color as yours?"

"Yep."

"Did I ever tell you what your mother used to say as a joke? She used to say she married me for my red hair."

"She did?"

"As a joke. I can hear her laugh yet."

"You can?"

"She was what you'd call a good-natured woman. Took things in her stride, like Jemmy. Except Jemmy hardly ever jokes."

"I don't like to scrape paint. Can I go help Marty?"

"Go ahead."

Candy dropped her paint scraper and ran to the half acre behind the shed, where Marty was digging post holes.

That evening after supper, Miss Frost showed up in her silver car. She came into the kitchen.

"The Chapmans want to know what your plans are, Jemmy. They called me. They said you were supposed to call them Sunday night."

"I decided not to."

"Well, what are your plans? Are you riding down with us, or are you going on the bus?"

"I decided not to go at all."

"What, not see your own picture dedicated by the governor?"

"I decided to stay home."

"For heaven's sake," said Miss Frost, looking puzzled. "Well, I suppose you have your reasons." She went out and got into her car and roared away.

On Wednesday morning as they scraped paint from the shed, Jemmy said to her father, "I want to know something."

"What?"

"Are you still drinking every day?"

"I have a drink of vodka in the evening, in my room."

"Is that all? One drink?"

"One's enough. One big one. It really hits the spot."

"I thought maybe you had cured yourself."

"Cured myself of what?"

"Alcoholism."

"I ain't no alcoholic. I can step up my drinking or I can tone it down, just as I please. I can go on a toot or lie low. I can quit—or almost quit—whenever I want to."

"Then what about last Sunday? What was all that noise I heard in your room?"

"That was my mistake. I was trying to quit altogether. I should have known better. It's pure agony to quit altogether. Then to top it off the Chapmans came into the house and camped in the kitchen and I couldn't make a peep. I felt like a prisoner in my own bedroom."

"Maybe you should try quitting again. Maybe if you're down to one drink a day you can quit completely. If you try."

Stott smelled a lecture. He took his scraper around to another wall and kept the shed between himself and Jemmy for the rest of the day.

On Thursday Jemmy drove to Eagleton to exchange the red paint for white and to see, in the public library, what the Minneapolis *Tribune* had to say about the dedication. On the front page was a picture of Otis shaking hands with the governor. They were standing in the Tower Courtyard. The mural was fuzzy in the background. "A triumphant addition to the cultural climate of our state," the article said. "A graphic reminder of our heritage."

Jemmy tried to make out the shapes in the mural but they were out of focus. Returning the newspaper to its rack, she was approached by the librarian, a bony woman of great height, who asked if she had seen the item about the mural.

"Yes, I did."

"Do you realize that it depicts our very own Eagle Rock?"

"Yes."

"And did you know that Otis Chapman himself was living in this area for a time, making sketches? And that his model for the Maiden was a girl from around here?"

"Yes, I knew that."

"He came into this library one day. He stood at that very desk. In the flesh. I checked out a book to him."

"You must have been thrilled," said Jemmy.

Leaving Eagleton, Jemmy drove past the high school. The clock on the dashboard said nine twenty-five. That meant first-hour history was almost over, to the relief of Mr. Olson. Jemmy pictured him in the classroom, tugging at his lapels, imploring his children to pay attention. Children? Why did she think of her former classmates as children? And why did her dropping out seem so long ago that she could recall only a few details of her last day? She remembered smoking in the rest room and cleaning out her locker, and then the blizzard came down like a curtain in a play, marking the division between acts. It marked the division between her high school days, fuzzy now in her memory, and what had happened since, all of it clear and sharp as the morning after a blizzard.

At home her father opened a can of white paint and

applied the first brushful to the weathered siding. Jemmy picked up a brush and worked at his side.

"She'll need two coats," he said. The weathered grain of the wood drank in the paint and dulled it.

"I want to take the Dodge to Minneapolis," said Jemmy. "I want to see the mural."

"The Dodge ain't ever been to Minneapolis."

"Neither have Marty and Candy. I'll go on Saturday and take them along."

"What about gas? That's at least two tanks of gas, down and back."

"I've got money. I got paid for being the model."

"And oil. You better take two or three extra quarts of oil along."

"All right."

"And there's one headlight burned out. You better get down there and back before dark, or you'll get picked up by the cops."

"We'll leave early."

Chapter 12

J emmy, Marty, and Candy left home at sunrise, traveling slowly because the Dodge shimmied at speeds over fifty. When they stopped along the way for breakfast, Jemmy said they could order whatever they wanted. She had brought some of her hundred and eighty dollars along.

"I want oatmeal and cocoa," Candy told the waitress.

"I want pancakes and pie," said Marty. "And a cigarette."

As they neared Minneapolis, the road map became too complex to follow, and Jemmy drove into the town of Anoka and parked behind the bus station. She bought three round-trip tickets into the city. On the bus Candy sat next to a lady who read her the funnies in the morning paper, and Jemmy sat next to a man whose breath was bad. Marty sat behind the driver, watched his every move, and got off the bus convinced that he had discovered his vocation in life.

On the city streets the Stotts clung tightly together. They passed through a revolving door into the Tower Courtyard, a spacious, domed expanse of shops, sunshine, potted plants, lunch wagons, and intersecting streams of people.

And above them was the mural. Jemmy's monumental image looked down at the three Stotts (their first reaction was something like astonishment, a drawing in of the breath), and it looked down at hundreds of shoppers whose paths and voices interwove, reminding Jemmy of Eagleton High School between classes.

"It's nice," said Candy, gazing up at the mural.

"It's weird," said Marty, intimidated by the size of his sister's image.

Jemmy looked about her. She had been shy about entering the Courtyard, afraid of causing a fuss when people recognized her as the Maiden, but now she saw that there was no such danger. Though many people paused to study the mural, not a single person in the Courtyard looked into the face of his fellow man. Everyone seemed unapproachable, avoiding eye contact, lost in his private thoughts. It was spooky to be at the center of all this humanity yet feel so utterly ignored. Jemmy tried, and failed, to remember a time when her sense of separation from others had been this intense. Not even in the forest during the blizzard had she been so alone. At least in the forest she had had the memory of her mother to guide her. But this place, where her mother had never been, was like a foreign country.

Marty and Candy grew restless, and when Jemmy released them they sprang away like birds. They popped in and out of stores and they bought popsicles and popcorn. On the escalator they made three dozen trips to the mezzanine.

Jemmy sat down on a bench and gave herself up to the mural, entering it as deeply as Otis must have done while painting it. She could see why he called it his supreme work. For his future's sake, and for Ann's, she hoped it wasn't, but how could he ever hope to equal this? It was true, as Ann had said, that you could almost smell autumn in the soft warm colors—the orange and green of maple and pine, the rose light in the sky and water, the golden haze hanging over the boulders along the river. And high above the cliff, riding the air with outstretched wings, was an eagle.

Next, her eyes were caught by the retreating brave, who

looked over his shoulder at the Maiden. Something about his face struck Jemmy as familiar. From this distance—the length of the Courtyard—she couldn't be sure but the eyes of the brave were reminiscent of someone she had known, someone now just beyond her memory.

Looking at the Maiden was like looking into a gigantic mirror. A few strands of the Maiden's hair were tangled on her shoulders and Jemmy caught herself impulsively lifting her hand to straighten them. Having been placed at the center of a legend for all time, she wondered how she could ever again be simply Jemmy Stott. Even if she was Jemmy to herself and her family she would remain the Maiden to millions. Well, she had been two people before. In high school she had been an Indian in the morning and a white in the afternoon. Some days, even now, she felt more Indian than white. And some days, facing Miss Frost or Roxanne, she felt more white than Indian. There was nothing so difficult about being two people if you didn't fight it.

Weren't most people really two people after all? Her father had the reputation of a worthless drinker; yet Jemmy now knew that he was concerned, in his frail way, with the welfare of his children. Her father was without pride, said Otis; yet Jemmy had seen the pride he took in a well-painted wall, a well-planted fencepost. At this very moment he might be painting the house or he might be lying drunk on the couch. Unlike the two sides of Jemmy, her father's two sides seemed to be locked in a continual struggle against each other.

And so did Ann's two sides. Ann supported her husband in his art, but only up to a point. Then another Ann took over—a wife who grew jealous of his art, who found fault with his dedication. How it must have hurt Otis when Ann, in her fit of annoyance, told him this mural was only paint and plaster.

And how many people was Otis? According to Ann, there was Otis the lovable and Otis the forbidding—though

Jemmy had never seen this latter Otis. Nor had she ever seen Otis the drunk, who was hidden—forever, she hoped—behind the black beard.

The black beard!

Jemmy leaped off the bench and pushed her way through throngs of people and stood directly under the retreating brave. The brave's face, without the beard and looking younger by several years, was the face she had seen in Ann's photo album—Otis's face. She was overcome by conflicting currents of loss and joy. Loss of Otis. Loss of Ann. And yet joy at having Otis looking back at her, remembering.

She had a sudden urge to tell somebody. She felt that only by speaking could she relieve the ache building up in her throat. She wanted to point out the message in the mural that all of Minneapolis was missing. She wanted to tell these two women in cream-colored slacks and this man carrying a briefcase that besides portraying the legend of the Maiden, this mural commemorated the six-month friendship between artist and model. Not only the Maiden, but Jemmy herself, was the subject of this mural. But how do you convey your joy—and your loss—to people who do not see you? Anyhow, this wasn't the sort of thing a girl told to strangers. It was the sort of thing a girl might tell her mother and no one else.

And so the ache in Jemmy's throat was unrelieved as she and Marty and Candy made their way back to the bus depot and sat, very tired now, in the waiting room. On the bus, in heavy traffic, moving away by fits and starts from the center of the city, Jemmy's sense of loss—her loss of the Chapmans—came to outweigh her gladness, and the ache spread upward from her throat and came to rest behind her eyes. It was the same stinging emotion she had felt when she was eleven and standing at her mother's open grave with a powerful urge to cry—an urge she overcame that gloomy day by keeping her eyes on her father, who seemed unmoved, and on Marty, who didn't grasp what was happening—an urge she overcame now by turning her gaze out the bus window and holding her hands up in the shape of a frame and imagining pictures that might be composed of the busy streets and the crowds of people and the endless blocks of buildings.

The orange sun was going down as they stepped off the bus in Anoka and got into the Dodge. Jemmy followed the highway out of town and drove barely a mile before Marty and Candy fell asleep, and barely ten miles before she was stopped by a highway patrolman. In exchange for Jemmy's promise to have the headlight repaired, the patrolman issued her not a traffic citation but merely a warning ticket.

She drove on, and as she put distance between herself and the city, as the trees multiplied and became forests silhouetted against the darkening gold of the evening sky, Jemmy's sense of loss gradually diminished. The Chapmans were gone, but they were leaving a lot behind. They were leaving Socko and they had promised to leave the portrait of the Maiden. They had helped to make a painter out of Jemmy and a painter—once again—out of her father. They had doted on Candy and they had helped Marty through the winter of his despair. All this in six months. To say nothing of the difference they had made in Jemmy's view of life. From the Chapmans she had learned much more than simply how to paint. She had learned to step back once in a while and look at her life through a frame. She had learned to understand her family better, particularly her father. She had learned much more about the nature of friendship than Roxanne could ever teach her. And she had come to understand what her mother had meant about the friendship of nature. It might be a long time now before someone came along to take the Chapmans' place in Jemmy's heart, but until that happened she would find other steadfast companions. She would pay more attention to the balance in trees. She would try to imitate the grace of eagles.

There was little traffic in the North. Mile after mile, the Dodge was alone on the highway, its single headlight moving home through the night.

The next morning Jemmy got up in the dark. She dressed and hurried outside to the Dodge, and as she drove away from the yard the sky came alight with the first pink flush of dawn. She passed the Chapmans' farm and saw the word *Sold* clipped to the realtor's sign. She followed the winding road through the forest—past the stone foundation, past the *Mean Dog* sign—and she arrived at Eagle Rock just as the tip of the sun flamed above the horizon. She drove only partway up the hill, then she left the car and walked through the dew-wet weeds. She moved stealthily, as though sneaking up on something. She reached the crest and cautiously approached the edge of the cliff and looked down at the rocks along the river. Like Otis, she felt she could point to the very stone upon which the Maiden, drained of hope, had destroyed herself.

The sun lifted itself up from the horizon, but Jemmy kept her eyes down, examining the outcroppings on the face of the cliff beneath her—the ledges of shale and the twisted bushes where eagles might nest. She stood there trancelike for several minutes until suddenly—startled—she saw what she had come for—a golden eagle bursting out from the face of the cliff in a flurry of loud wingbeats. The great bird climbed high over the river, high over Jemmy, then dipped and banked, leveled off and sailed over the rooftops of Eagleton, almost vanishing—only to return on a buoyant updraft of air that carried it high over Jemmy's head. There it hovered motionless for several seconds; then it dropped and circled, dropped and circled, riding out and back over the river in seven circles at seven levels, gliding gracefully all the while—and finally soaring away on the strong currents of the upper air, riding far off and out of sight on the winds of sunrise.

Jemmy's heart pounded with excitement. She closed her eyes and swayed slightly from side to side as she committed to memory the pattern of the eagle's flight. She felt the breeze in her hair and the warm sun on her cheek and the stony ground underfoot, and she felt herself a part of these things—as though by climbing to this sacred height she had transcended her other life of cleaning and cooking and washing clothes and had become one with the elements of nature, one with the sky and the wind and the turning globe.

Slowly, she opened her eyes, like someone emerging from a dream.

She felt refreshed.

She turned and went down the hill to the car.

She drove home to make breakfast for her family.

ABOUT THE AUTHOR

Jon Hassler was born in Minnesota in 1933. He began his teaching career in 1955 and is currently writer-in-residence at St. John's University, Minnesota. His first novel, STAGGERFORD, was published in 1977 and was followed by SIMON'S NIGHT, THE LOVE HUNTER, A GREEN JOURNEY, GRAND OPENING, and two novels for young adults, JEMMY and FOUR MILES TO PINECONE.

MORE POPULAR THAN EVER

Isabelle Holland